WINNING THE COWBOY BILLIONAIRE

A CHAPPELL BROTHERS NOVEL: BLUEGRASS RANCH ROMANCE BOOK 1

EMMY EUGENE

Copyright © 2020 by Emmy Eugene

All rights reserved.

No part of this book may be reproduced in any form or by any electronic or mechanical means, including information storage and retrieval systems, without written permission from the author, except for the use of brief quotations in a book review.

ISBN-13: 979-8687691864

CHAPTER 1

Olivia Hudson smoothed down the dress she wore, though it would never lay completely flat against her stomach. She carried about twenty-five extra pounds, and no matter how much she tried to lose the barrel around her waistline, it wouldn't go.

Perhaps she didn't try that hard. She did spend a lot of time on her feet, looking for new herbs, plants, and fruits to make into oils and fragrances for her handmade, deluxe perfumes. She distilled everything in her very own perfumery, and every bottle got a fancy gold and pink sticker that Olli had designed herself. She even peeled and stuck the stickers onto the bottles herself.

Virginia helped, of course. Olli's best friend helped with everything, including getting her this invitation to a wedding in Chestnut Springs, Texas.

Olli didn't know Theo Lange or Sorrell Adams, but Theo was Virginia's half-brother. Olli could still remember when

Ginny had found out and how upset she'd been. To Olli's knowledge, Ginny hadn't spent much time with Theo at all; they never spoke; no attempt had been made to welcome him into the Winters family.

Olli knew how hard it was to break into the Winters inner circle, that was for sure. She'd been friends with Ginny for three years before she'd even been invited over to the sprawling mansion surrounded by huge barley, rye, wheat, and corn fields.

The Winters owned an old and reputable whiskey distillery in Kentucky, and Olli had a lot of respect for their family even if Ginny's father had been extremely difficult to deal with.

Theo was apparently one of his illegitimate children, and yet Ginny and her mother had chosen to attend his wedding. Olli threw a look to Wendy Winters, and the woman was poised and proper, as always.

Olli often wanted to be more like her, but she simply couldn't do it. She loved to laugh, and she liked to drive around horse country with the top down on her old Mustang, breathing in the scent of fresh grass, pure sunshine, and the distinct scent of horses, hay, and dirt.

Today, though, there was no hay or dirt. Plenty of sunshine here in Texas in May, and lots of horses on this patch of land where they'd gathered for the wedding. But no dirt, as Theo had apparently inherited his father's good business sense and had a lot of money.

Ginny came into the room and scanned Olli. "You look

beautiful." She linked her arm through Olli's with a smile. "Let's go sit down."

Ginny was the one with pure beauty radiating from her high cheekbones, long limbs, and deep, nearly navy blue eyes. Olli giggled with her as they left the house and headed to the chairs that had been set up in the back garden.

The flowers and plants and grass bloomed earlier here in Texas than they did in Kentucky, and Olli's nose went into overdrive. "I want some of those flowers," she said, indicating a tall stalk with beautiful blooms protruding from each side of it every few inches. "Don't they smell amazing?"

"I thought you were working on masculine scents," Ginny said, steering Olli away from the flowers. She'd get a picture of them later, because she could then take that to her contact at the nursery, and he'd tell her what kind of flower it was.

"I am," Olli said. "I've got to break out of musk and pine." She glanced at a couple of cowboys who watched her and Ginny pass. She smiled at them, but she wasn't looking for a long-distance relationship. Olli wasn't looking for a relationship at all, unless one with a new investor for her perfumery counted.

She'd written and submitted four grants this year alone, and the waiting process could test even the most patient person. Heck, the Dalai Lama would probably find the process exhausting.

She sat, though, and she enjoyed the fans that blew from above in an attempt to keep the guests cool. Ginny's mother joined them, and a few moments later, the ceremony started to come together.

Theo, a tall, dark cowboy Olli might have found attractive once-upon-a-time took his place at the altar, a wide, hopeful smile on his face.

She'd felt like that once. Hopeful and happy about her romantic prospects. She'd dated plenty of men in her twenties and thirties. She'd even worn a diamond ring once. She'd vowed she never would again, though. Not after she'd made it all the way through the wedding preparations, the engagement pictures, the save-the-dates, the food sampling, and the formal pictures in the fields that surrounded her family farm.

She hadn't quite been stood up at the altar, but almost. Her fiancé had called the morning before the wedding, mere hours before the final rehearsal dinner. She'd invited her whole family to that. His too.

I can't do this, he'd said. *It has nothing to do with you, Olli. I swear.*

She almost scoffed right out loud at this wedding, five years later. She'd been in enough relationships to know that when one ended, it had something to do with her, even if her contribution was small.

She put her ex out of her mind as the wedding march started to play. Olli stood with the rest of the crowd, and she turned to watch the most beautiful woman walk down the aisle, one slow step at a time. She wasn't hanging on the arm of her father, obviously, as the man escorting her appeared to be about her same age.

Olli's curiosity lifted, as she loved getting to know people and learning their stories. Did she speak to her father? Was he alive? Too sick to walk her down the aisle? What was the story there?

Olli loved stories, and the more personal, the better. She could take those ideas and transform them into scents for her perfumes and candles, and she always found the best inspiration from real life.

She sighed as the bride moved past her, and she enjoyed watching Theo and Sorrell get married right there in their own back garden. She'd been resistant to coming to this wedding with Ginny, but Ginny had pulled the best friend card, and Olli had been helpless at that point.

She'd bought a new dress, packed a bag, and come to Texas, a state she'd never visited before.

"Sorrell," Theo said. "I've loved you for seven long years. Eight maybe." He ducked his head, and Olli sighed again, this time pressing her hand over her pulse. She'd always had a weakness for soft-yet-tough cowboys, and Theo seemed like exactly that type.

"I promise to love you and take care of you for the rest of my life." He looked up at her, the joy on his face something Olli wished she could bottle and sell.

Radiant joy, she thought. *Smells like sunshine, weddings, and...* She cast a look to that flower, thinking it would be perfect for her bright yellow Radiant Joy candle. The one she hadn't developed yet.

"Theo," Sorrell said. "You've shown more patience than any man I've ever met. I love you, and I'm grateful for you. I know we'll have an amazing life together, no matter what comes our way."

Olli couldn't help smiling as the pastor pronounced them man and wife, and Theo leaned down to kiss his new wife. She'd been to plenty of weddings in Kentucky, with plenty of cowboys, but the whooping and heehawing that erupted from this group was enough to startle her pulse into overdrive.

"My goodness," she said, looking at Ginny. They burst out laughing together, and Ginny leaned toward her.

She had to practically yell, "Texas cowboys are different than Kentucky cowboys, I guess," for Olli to hear her.

Olli looked around, thinking that they might be louder, but to her, the cowboys here looked and smelled and acted a lot like the ones she knew back home.

She was fine being friends with them. She just didn't want one coming into her life and trying to take over her business—or her heart—again.

* * *

"What do you mean?" she asked a few days later. "The grant didn't say anything about being married."

"You don't need to be married, Miss Hudson," the man on the other end of the line said, his tone somewhat rounded and clipped at the same time. He definitely wasn't from the South, and Olli wished her accent wasn't quite so thick. "Mister Renlund simply wants to make sure his investment is going to a family company."

Olli didn't know what to say. She'd missed that requirement in the grant application.

"He very much likes your proposal," Benjamin said,

continuing despite the tailspin Olli's thoughts had gone into. "He found it so different from what we usually get. You're on the list of his top five, and he comes around and visits everyone and their businesses before he decides on the grant money."

"You're kidding," Olli said, looking around. Her perfumery sat in a state of chaos at the moment, with vials and bottles all over the place. She'd learned the flower in Texas was called a gladiolus, and she'd already ordered several varieties to be delivered in the next week or so.

"I am not kidding, Miss Hudson," Benjamin said. "We're looking at being there in about two weeks. Does that work for you?"

Olli reached for her desk calendar, clearing away a couple of pieces of unopened mail, a pile of rubber bands, and a stack of unmade boxes for her sample bottles of perfumes. "Uh, two weeks?" That would put them in the third week of May. "How long will Mister Renlund want to be here?"

Would she have to house him? Show him around Lexington? Her mind raced with the possibilities, and she reminded herself that she was very personable. She'd worked as a tour guide on two horse farms in the area before achieving her dream of opening and operating her own perfumery.

"Only a few days, ma'am. I'll send you his itinerary. He'd love to meet your husband or boyfriend."

Olli sat back, her frustration morphing into anger. "What if I don't have a husband or boyfriend?"

"That's why I call in advance," Benjamin said. "If I were you, Miss Hudson, I'd get one, even for a few days. In two weeks' time."

She opened her mouth to respond, but she blanked.

"Good day," Benjamin said, and the call ended. Olli scoffed as she took the phone from her ear and checked to make sure he'd hung up.

"Unbelievable," she muttered to herself. "That guy lives in the eighteen hundreds." Didn't he know women could—and did—run their own businesses these days?

No man needed.

Olli stared out the window across the room from her desk, trying to think of a single man she could somehow convince to be her boyfriend for a few days.

She'd grown up here in the Lexington area, and she knew a lot of people, but the only men who came to her mind were the Chappell brothers.

They owned Bluegrass Ranch, which happened to be located right next door to Olli's place. She saw at least five of them ride by her window on any given day of the week.

She stood up and went to the window, looking left and right as if one of them would happen upon her and offer her a diamond ring. One didn't.

Her stomach writhed, but no one else had called about any of the other grants. Two of them had rejected her on the same day yesterday, in fact.

Desperation clogged in her throat, and it wasn't pleasant. She squared her shoulders and started for the door. She could go next door and see what was happening with the Chappells. In the back of her mind, she thought she'd heard that a couple of them had started dating someone recently.

There were eight to choose from. It couldn't be that hard

to get one of the boys next door to be her arm candy for a few days.

Olli stopped by the door of her perfumery and picked up a bottle of her newest scent, Seduction.

"Perfect," she muttered, spritzing the perfume on her neck and mostly bare shoulders. "Game on, boys."

She left the perfumery and looked to the road that ran east and west in front of her workshop. Her windows faced south, and she'd seen someone go by about a half an hour ago.

"What are you going to do? Stand on the side of the road and flag him down?" She didn't even know who she'd get next.

She decided it didn't matter, as long as it was one of the older Chappell brothers. She was forty-four, and she knew Cayden Chappell was her same age.

"No problem," she said. She didn't have Cayden's number, but she had Spur's. He was the oldest brother, and they'd exchanged numbers years ago when she'd first moved in next door.

"Just in case," he'd said.

Olli hadn't known what that had meant at the time, but she did now. Just in case his cattle got out. Just in case his horses broke through a fence. Just in case the Chappells had to turn off the water to the whole street—which was just their place and hers—for some ranch construction. Just in case he had to tell her the big rigs would be coming to get the horses they'd sold. Just in case he needed the field she owned between their places for all of his high rollers to park.

There had been a lot of instances of *just in case* over the years with Spur Chappell.

She'd spoken to Spur on all of those occasions. He rarely wore a smile, and though she'd known him for years, he still intimidated her.

So definitely Cayden, she told herself, still standing just outside the perfumery, which sat a hop, skip, and jump from her front door. Foolishness rushed through her, and she couldn't get herself to take a single step.

A loud whistle rent the country silence, and Olli whipped her attention toward the sound.

She became aware of dogs barking, and the thundering of horse hooves, and another earsplitting whistle. "Ho, there," a man yelled, and Olli watched as Spur Chappell rode right in front of her on a magnificent bay horse.

She fell backward at the sudden appearance of him, realizing that he'd put himself between her and an oncoming herd of sheep.

A scream came from her mouth as she steadied herself against the door, and then Spur rode in front of her again, yipping and yelling at someone or something else. The dogs kept barking and barking, and just like someone had put up an invisible fence, the swarm of sheep turned away from her and the perfumery and went in a wide arc toward the south.

Olli pressed her palm over her heartbeat, watching the fifty or so sheep flow away from her.

The dogs went with them, but Spur himself turned and looked at Olli, their eyes meeting and locking for what felt like forever.

A grin danced across his face, and he lifted one gloved

hand and acknowledged her before pressing his cowboy hat further onto his head and galloping after the sheep.

"Oh, my..." Olli let her words hang there, all of her focus now on the handsome cowboy who would look *mighty* fine on her arm for just one night.

CHAPTER 2

S pur Chappell hated sheep with everything in him. They had a special talent for getting out of their fences, though they literally had the smallest brains of all farm animals.

He hated that they even had sheep at Bluegrass Ranch, but his youngest brother had insisted he get them. Spur had wanted to keep Duke on at the ranch, and he'd given in.

He wished now that he'd listened to his intuition, which had told him these sheep would be more trouble than they were worth. Not only that, but that Duke would not be around to tend to them properly.

He was off in Alabama this week, looking at two new mares he wanted to bring to the ranch, and that meant Spur was the one in the saddle with all the cattle dogs, trying to round up the naughty sheep.

Things happened swiftly from time to time, and he hadn't had a spare second to call or text Olivia Hudson, his next-door neighbor, and warn her about the sheep. There were only five dozen or so, but sheep could cause some damage if they were left unchecked.

Of course, they'd headed straight for her place the moment he'd swung into the saddle. Double of course, she'd been standing outside, waiting to be trampled.

He knew they wouldn't do that, but he'd still put himself and his dogs between the herd and the woman, because the last thing he and Bluegrass Ranch needed was a lawsuit.

Twenty minutes later, he had all the sheep back in their corral, where Blaine had fixed the fences they'd broken through. He touched his hand to his hat for his brother and called, "I have to go talk to Olli. They gave her a fright."

Blaine waved to indicate he'd heard Spur, and Spur set his sights on his one and only neighbor out here in the hills beyond Lexington. He loved the land out here, which always seemed to be made of emerald green grass and bright white fences. He loved the sky when it was pure blue, and when it had puffy clouds in it, and when the wind blew in a storm.

He loved the smell of fresh water in the stream on his land, and the scent of sawdust in the air from the new bridges he'd just put in.

His horse breathed rapidly, and Spur leaned down to pat All Out's neck. "Good boy," he said to the horse, the way one would to a dog. "We got 'em, thanks to you."

It was the dogs who'd really done most of the herding work, but Spur never told the horses that. His horses all believed they were kings and queens, because he raised them to be. They had championship blood in their veins, and he expected them to train and run like it.

That was how he made his money, after all. If he had a horse who wasn't a diva and couldn't run, he couldn't do anything with that horse. His family ranch depended on breeding and selling top-quality horses that would run until the day they dropped dead.

Not that Spur ever pushed them that far. But he had seen over a dozen of the horses he'd bred and sold win the Belmont, the Kentucky Derby, or the Preakness. Two of his horses had won all three in the same year, taking that Triple Crown.

Every time one of his horses won, any horse in that bloodline got more valuable. Spur kept immaculate records of the horse races around the world, and when he walked into an auction, everyone took note.

The woman next door didn't care about any of that, though, and Spur brought his ego back down to Earth as he went up the road to her house. He found her outside still, down on her hands and knees as she ripped up the flowers his sheep had trampled.

She heard him coming, and she got to her feet and wiped her sun kissed hair off her forehead. She cocked one hip while he brought All Out to a stop and swung out of the saddle.

"Hey, Olli," he said, walking toward her so he could see the damage in her flower garden.

"Spur," she said, clearly not happy with him.

"Sorry about the sheep." They'd done a number on whatever she'd had growing there. "Tell me how much to fix that."

"You can't fix that," she said. "Those were my gardenias

and a new crop of four o'clocks. I use that gardenia for my Down Home South candle." She glared at him.

"I'm sorry," he said, and he meant it. "Animals are unpredictable."

She took a step toward him, and he wouldn't have predicted she'd do that. His heartbeat skipped over itself for a moment, and he wasn't even sure why. He'd talked to Olli lots of times; she was pretty in a Southern belle kind of way, though he'd never let himself think about her for too long.

He hadn't let himself entertain thoughts about a woman for years now, though if he had, he could easily see himself fantasizing about the curvy, gorgeous Olivia Hudson.

She was still prowling toward him, something sparking in her eyes that interested him. Maybe he had thought a lot about Olli and had just never admitted it to himself. He pushed against the idea now too.

"I can pay for the damage," he said, clearing his throat as her perfume hit his nose. She smelled amazing, like lemons and vanilla and cookies. He wanted a taste of her right then, and he couldn't believe himself.

"I can have one of my men come replant the flowers," he said, sticking to facts to keep his brain in control of this situation. "I know they won't be good enough or ready when you need them, but I'm not sure what else to do to make it right."

Olli stopped a couple of feet from him and looked him up and down. Spur suddenly wished he wasn't sweaty and dusty from rounding up the sheep. He held his ground, glad when her eyes finally returned to his.

"Sorry, Olli," he said again, wishing she'd name her price so he could go.

"You can do all of that," she said. "And I need one more favor, Spur."

"Name it," he said. "Along with the monetary amount, Olli."

"It'll be hundreds to pull out the ruined plants and put them in again." She switched her gaze to the flower garden, which was huge. Just how big Spur hadn't realized. He reminded himself that she ran a perfumery, and she grew most of the stuff she used to produce the fragrances herself.

"Include your lost product," he said. "I want to pay for that too."

"You will," she said. "I'll have to do some estimates."

"You have my number." He started to turn away from her magnetic gaze, telling himself not to ask her out right now. He couldn't even believe he was *thinking* about asking her out. His mother would be thrilled he was "getting back on the horse" again, but Spur wasn't.

He wasn't interested in dating. He *wasn't*. He simply couldn't admit his interest in Olli to himself. He first needed to figure out how long he'd be interested in her.

"Spur," she said, her voice even and calm.

"Hmm?" He looked back at her, unable to just walk away. Not while she wore that pale blue tank top and those denim shorts. Her hair fell in soft waves over her shoulders, and Spur just wanted to brush it back so he could feel her skin there, breathe in the scent of her, and kiss her.

He struggled to get control of his thoughts as she started speaking.

"Probably a thousand for the plants. Send over your guys to get this cleaned up and replanted." She cocked her head. "I'll text you about the lost product."

He nodded, something anchoring him in place. Maybe he didn't want to leave yet, but he couldn't fathom why he'd need to stay.

"The favor is that I need you to be my boyfriend for a few days," Olli said, holding his gaze with strength in her shoulders and back.

Spur stared at her, the words she'd said swimming through his whole system. He started laughing, because she couldn't be serious.

She smiled too, and Spur relaxed. She was just teasing him, something she'd done before when one of his studs had gotten out and kicked a hole through her storage shed. Then, she'd said she'd like to hire *him* out for a stud fee, and they'd had a good laugh together.

Today, though, she didn't join him, and he cut his laughter off pretty quickly. "I'll see who I have available to come do this," he said. "Could be a day or two."

"The party is in a couple of weeks," she said. "Might not even be a party. But you'll need to look nice, and wear that cowboy hat that you wear to church, and a pair of boots that you haven't worn on the ranch." She dropped her eyes to his current pair of cowboy boots, and Spur's pulse kicked at his ribs now.

"Party?" he practically growled.

"I have an investor interested in funding my business," she said, a slight frown appearing between her eyes. "He's very... traditional, and I've been told I need a husband or a boyfriend. A serious boyfriend." Those perfectly sculpted eyebrows went up, as if to ask him *Do you catch my drift, Spur?*

He caught it. He wasn't sure if he wanted to fist it tight and hold it close or throw it right back in her face.

"Dear Lord, you're not kidding," he said.

"I am not," she said, taking another step toward him. "It'll be for a few days at the most, Spur. It's a lot of money, and I need it."

His first instinct was to tell her he'd give her whatever money she needed. He had plenty of money, and not much time or patience for parties or small talk. Cayden, his next youngest brother was the public relations director for the horse breeding ranch. He was the one who cleaned up nice and entertained their buyers and sellers.

Spur had never cleaned his boots for a girlfriend, real or fake.

What if she wasn't fake? he thought, and he had no idea where that had come from.

"Okay," he said, just as surprised as Olli. He managed to keep his eyebrows down while hers went up again.

"Really?" she asked.

"It's a few days, right?" he asked. "I just ruined a lot more work than that. I can wear a clean pair of boots and a nice hat for a few days."

"You'd just hang on my arm," she said with a smile. "Charm the socks off of the investor. It'll be easy."

Spur had never hung on anyone's arm, nor did he have much charm, so he didn't think it would be that easy, but he refrained from rolling his eyes. "Just tell me when," he said, taking the steps away from her that he needed to clear his head.

"I'll text you," she said, and Spur got himself back in the saddle, waved, and went back to Bluegrass Ranch.

Along the way, All Out nickered, as if asking Spur what in the world he'd been thinking.

"I don't know," he muttered as he arrived at the row house and started unsaddling the horse. What he did know was that Olli hadn't left his mind in the past twenty minutes, and that he couldn't get the tantalizing scent of her out of his nose.

He hadn't even known he had a crush on the woman, but his heart was testifying differently. Surprise accompanied Spur as he took care of his horse and put away the equipment he'd used.

He hadn't thought he'd ever want another girlfriend in his life, not after the break-up of his first marriage. He'd been stuck on Katie for a long time after the divorce was final, and he'd never started dating again, though he probably could have five years ago.

"I never saw the point," he said to All Out as he gave the horse a bag of oats. "Is there a point to this?"

All Out snickered at him again, and Spur grinned at the horse. "No candy, boy. All we did was ride after some sheep." He stroked the horse's neck as he thought about Olli.

"I can't believe we can trick an investor if we don't get together beforehand," he said to the horse, seizing onto his own words. He pulled out his phone and called Olli, always preferring to just talk rather than text.

"Spur," she said, clear surprise in her voice.

"Heya, Olli," he drawled. "I was just thinking...this investor is probably pretty savvy. What's your plan for convincing him that we're a real couple?"

She didn't respond, and that was all the answer Spur needed. A smile touched his mouth again. "Do you want to go to dinner tonight? I feel like maybe we should get some facts in line before we have to convince anyone we're together."

"Facts?" she asked.

"Yeah," he said. "Wouldn't your boyfriend know a bit about your business? And maybe your middle name? Facts."

"Dinner tonight," she mused.

"I'm free every night this week," he said, wishing he could recall the words the moment he said them. He pressed his eyes closed, wondering if he'd just given away too much of what he was really feeling. As he waited for her to answer, he finally admitted to himself that he'd noticed Olli's pretty hair and quick smile years ago. He'd just shoved the feelings away whenever they came, and maybe now he wouldn't.

"I can go to dinner tonight," she said.

"I'll wear the right hat and boots," he said. "You can check me off piece by piece."

She laughed, and said, "Okay, Spur. Seven?"

"See you at seven," he said. The call ended, and Spur just stood there, staring down the row of stalls where he kept his champions. "Who knew asking a woman out would be so easy?"

"Who'd you ask out?" Blaine asked, coming up behind Spur. "Momma's gonna freak out."

Spur flinched, because Blaine wasn't wrong. "It's nothing," he said. "Who have we got to send over to Olli's to fix her flower garden?"

Blaine sighed and shrugged. "I don't know. We're swamped over here, Spur."

They were, and Spur knew it. He put a growl on his face and in his voice when he said, "Fine, I'll do it," but he couldn't quite get himself to be unhappy about being able to go next door to see the woman again.

Dealing with his mother would be another issue, and Spur really *wasn't* looking forward to that. Thankfully, he usually only saw her on Sundays, and he still had five days before he'd have to face her.

Plenty of time to figure out if something with Olli could be real or if he'd just pretend to be her boyfriend so she could get the funding she needed. Then he could go back to pretending he hadn't thought about her in a romantic way.

You're such a liar, he told himself, but if Olli wasn't truly interested in him, Spur wouldn't open his heart for her to put new gashes on.

He knew better than that.

CHAPTER 3

"Spur Chappell?" Ginny said the moment Olli opened her front door.

"Shh." Olli reached for her and ushered her inside, as if one of the other Chappell brothers would be standing there, watching. Eavesdropping. The Chappells also had dozens and dozens of cowboys and cowgirls who came to Bluegrass Ranch to work with the horses there. They had their own practice track and everything, and they seemed to have activity at the ranch from sunup to sundown.

"Shh?" Ginny repeated. "Their ranch is at least a mile from here." She looked at Olli with her sharp, navy eyes. She'd learned her pointed look from her picture-perfect mother, and Olli hated being on the receiving end of it.

"I just don't think you need to shout his name out here." She stepped past her friend, ignoring the state of her kitchen and living room. She wasn't the best housekeeper on the planet, but no one she lived with cared. Witcher, the hermit cat she shared the house with, probably liked the obstacles Olli left behind. "Now, come on. I need help with my outfit."

"So you like him," Ginny asked, following Olli past the couch where she'd slept last night, the dining room table filled with notebooks with ideas, bottles, boxes, and her business computer, and a basket of clean laundry Olli had been picking through for a week now.

"No," Olli said with a scoff, though she heard a bit of a false note in her own voice. "I just want to dress to impress." She indicated the three outfits she'd spent the last hour putting together.

"Because he's rich."

That was one reason, though Olli had never cared to impress Spur or any of the other Chappell men before. "Because I need this to work," she said, really adding some bite to her words to drive home her point. "What if we fight all night? Or he decides I'm disgusting, and he can't even pretend to be my boyfriend?" She shook her head. "I *need* this to work, Ginny."

Ginny appraised her for another moment. "Okay, but let's be clear. One, he *is* rich."

"Fine," Olli conceded. "He's rich."

"Two," Ginny said, her eyes and voice growing more animated. "You want to look like the type of woman a man like him would have on his arm, which of course you are, because you're *not* disgusting. Three, he's drop-dead gorgeous. Even you can't deny that. Four, you want this to work so you can win over the investor coming into town in a couple of weeks. Five, you haven't had a boyfriend in a while and you're nervous. Six—"

"Enough," Olli finally said, adding a laugh to it. "Yes to all of that, and anything else you were going to say. He's going to be here in thirty minutes. I need you to pick out the outfit and help me with my hair."

"Your hair is already flawless." Ginny stepped over to the bed and started examining the slacks, skirts, and blouses Olli had laid out. "You don't even know what point six was going to be."

"Probably something about how I'll consider him for my real boyfriend if the date goes well," Olli said, rolling her eyes. "You sometimes forget that I've known you for twenty years."

"I do not," Ginny said, picking up the black blouse with tiny white horses on it. She handed it to Olli with a dry spark in her eyes. "I've been picking out clothes for you for two decades, and it has been *taxing*."

Olli laughed, and Ginny joined in as she went back to the bed. "If you hate it so much, then why do you keep coming over when I call?"

"Someone has to look like a million bucks when they go out."

"You could have any man you wanted," Olli said. "You just have to say yes when one of them asks."

"No one asks," Ginny said. She turned back with the denim pencil skirt in her hand. Olli had been secretly hoping she'd pick that, because she did think it showed off her curvy hips but skinny legs.

"You're such a liar," Olli said, taking the skirt. She started shimmying out of her leggings and into the skirt. "I know a man asked you out in Texas last week. You said no."

"Yeah, because he lives in *Texas*," Ginny said. "Not sure if you remember, Olls, but we live in Kentucky. The two states don't even touch each other."

"He was really cute," Olli said. "You could've flown in or something."

Ginny scoffed and went back to the apparel on the bed. "You need big hoops with that blouse. Silver. You should wear that black opal your mother gave you too."

"Okay," Olli said, switching out her gardening T-shirt for the blouse. "Front tuck? Back? All around?"

"Front," Ginny said, stepping over to Olli and tucking in the blouse for her. She tugged some of it back out and stood back. "Amazing. Shoes." She turned back to the bed, where Olli had laid no less than seven pairs of shoes and sandals, wedges and ankle boots. "None of these."

"None of those?" Olli stepped over to her dresser and started rummaging for the ring and earrings Ginny had suggested. "Those are the best ones I have."

"No, you have that pair of black sandals with the skinny straps."

"Those are barely shoes," Olli said. She hated them too, because they were completely flat, and her arches hurt after the first hour.

"They're sexy," Ginny said.

"They barely stay on."

Ginny didn't answer, and once Olli secured her jewelry in

place, she turned to find Ginny on her hands and knees, digging through Olli's closet.

"Ginny," she said. "You don't have to do that. Even those ankle boots would be fine." She looked at the black leather with the small heel. Spur was plenty tall, and she could definitely wear a heel with him.

"I would never allow you to even be buried in those ankle boots," Ginny said from within the closet. "They're hideous. They should be burned."

A sting moved through Olli's chest. She picked up the ankle boots and looked at them, finding them cute. They'd been affordable too, and when she'd worn them to church, one of the ladies had said she liked them.

Yeah, Olli thought. *She was eighty years old, Olli.*

She put down the possibly ugly boots and looked at Ginny as she emerged from the closet. She stood up and showed Olli the pair of bright blue pumps she held. "These."

"No way," Olli said. "Those were the stupid shoes for Bethany's wedding. I hated them."

"No," Ginny said. "We hated those bridesmaids dresses. Those were also hideous, but *these* are perfect." She polished them up using the hem on her bright white blouse—which hadn't rumpled despite her search through the closet—and placed them on the floor. "Just try them."

Olli sighed like Ginny was making her wear snakes on her feet and stepped into the shoes. She did like wearing heels, because she thought they gave her calves some definition in the muscle. The blue and the denim went well together, and the bright color somehow seemed to make the black blouse more exciting.

"Okay, you win," she said to Ginny.

"This is why you call me," she said with a smile. "And why I come every time you do." She hugged Olli, and the two of them giggled together. She suddenly pulled back and searched Olli's face. "I just realized he has seven brothers. If this goes well, you could totally set me up with one of them."

Olli shook her head and stepped back from her best friend. "Ginny, you could get all seven of them to ask you out on your own."

Ginny didn't answer, and Olli turned to go into her bathroom. She didn't want to paint over her real face, so she'd kept her makeup fresh and light. She added more color to her lips and ran her fingers through her hair. "It's okay?" she asked as Ginny joined her.

"It's natural," she said, looking at Olli in the mirror. "Perfect. If you don't drive him wild with your hair alone, the rest of us have no hope whatsoever."

Olli laughed and shook her head. She had hair somewhere between the color of ripe wheat and the mahogany floors in her house. It did have a natural wave in it and fell several inches below her shoulders. It parted naturally above her right eye, a long, straight line that required little effort from her.

Her eyes fell to her midsection, cataloging all the faults to go with her perfect hair. Ginny had pretty perfect hair too, hers a much darker shade of brown that always looked like she'd glossed it so the sun would reflect off of it in the most brilliant way.

"Okay," Olli said, wishing she could lose twenty pounds in the next twenty minutes. "What else?"

"Purse? Wallet?"

"I'm just taking my cell phone," Olli said. "I've got my driver's license, credit card, and business card in the case."

Ginny rolled her eyes. "Business card. Come on, Olli. What are you going to do? Pitch the guy over steaks and seafood?"

Olli had already pitched him the idea of being her fake boyfriend. She knew the Chappells had money, and she hadn't thought of asking him to invest in her company. She wasn't going to do that tonight either. "I just never leave the house without one," she said. "That's all."

"You should lean in real close and find out what he smells like," Ginny said, her bright eyes dancing.

"Perfume." Olli snapped her fingers and moved down the cabinet, where at least a dozen bottles sat. "Tonight smells like…" She examined the bottles, trying to decide what she wanted tonight to be. Had this been a real date, she'd probably go with Seduction again. Or Nightberry, which was equal parts romance in the fruity undertones and mystery in the darker scents of Evening, Intrigue, and Spice.

"Wide Open," she said, selecting the bottle. It held Hope and Vulnerability in the fresh scents of honeysuckle and pink grapefruit, which were mostly masked by Possibilities, which she'd represented with the crisp scent of cotton. She spritzed the perfume along her collar, the insides of both wrists, and then up into the air. She stepped into the spray and let it fall into her hair before turning to look at Ginny.

"Ready?" her friend asked. "Oh, that does smell amazing."

"It's the hair spritz you need to remember," Olli said, handing her the bottle. "You should douse yourself in it and then go to that garden social tonight. I'm *sure* you'll meet someone there who'll ask you out."

Ginny rolled her eyes, "I'm not going to the garden social, I'm forty-five, not dead."

Olli laughed just as the doorbell rang. That peal cut off her laughter, and she met Ginny's eyes with plenty of fear running through her veins. She couldn't believe she'd been bold enough to ask Spur to be her fake boyfriend. She'd been even more surprised when he'd agreed. When he'd called to ask her out, Olli had sat at her perfumery desk for a solid twenty minutes afterward, wondering what in the world had just happened.

"Go on," Ginny hissed. "I'll stay back here and find some perfume to spritz in my hair." She gave Olli a little nudge, and that got Olli moving down the hall toward the front door.

She opened it a few seconds later to find Spur Chappell standing there, looking absolutely scrumptious in a pair of black slacks, polished and shined cowboy boots, a pale yellow shirt, open at the throat with a tie in brown, yellow, and blue knotted loosely around his neck. He wore a dark brown cowboy hat, and every single piece of him went together like magic.

"Heya, Olli," he said, his voice made of deep, dark waters, sweetened with honey. He looked down to her heels and back to her eyes. "You look amazing."

"Thanks," she managed to say. How had she never

acknowledged how handsome he was? His dark hair held plenty of silver in it, on both his head and his face. He smiled, his lips parting to reveal straight, white teeth. Everything about him screamed wealth and power, and Olli remembered how much he intimidated her.

"Do I pass?" he asked, turning in a slow circle. The man had no idea what he did to her pulse, and Olli contained it behind a smile of her own.

When their eyes met again, she shrugged one shoulder. "I suppose so. The hat is at least the one you wear to church."

"These boots are brand-new," he said. "Never worn on a ranch." He lifted one foot as if she couldn't see them herself.

"I like the half-tied necktie look too," she said, reaching up and flipping the bottom of his necktie. "Very cowboy casual."

"I can be buttoned up, if you'd like," he said, his fingers following hers and touching the tie, then his collar.

"No," she practically yelled. He looked at her again, something catching between them. She couldn't look away from him, and he couldn't seem to look away from her either. "I like it," she said, much quieter. "It's sexy."

"Sexy," Spur repeated, his eyes now dropping to her mouth. They rebounded so fast, Olli thought sure she'd hallucinated his eye movement. He wasn't thinking about kissing her. That would be an impossibility.

This was just dinner to get to know each other better, so they could trick the investor. Nothing more.

"Should we get going?" Spur asked, backing up a couple of steps.

She hadn't invited him in, and she said, "Yes, just a sec,"

and quickly retraced her steps to the kitchen counter to grab her phone-wallet. "I'm ready." She stepped outside and closed the door behind her, telling herself *nothing more, nothing more, nothing more* over and over again as she walked with him down the sidewalk to his truck.

CHAPTER 4

S pur decided Olli had called one of his brothers and asked them all of his favorite things. A face mostly without makeup. Check. Subdued colors. Check. The scent of crisp linen and something citrusy. Check. Heck, the woman even had horses on her blouse.

Every single thing about her called to Spur, and he had no idea what to do about it. He'd spent most of the day wondering why he'd never done anything about his feelings in the past, and he cursed—and praised—those silly sheep for bringing this date to fruition.

He opened Olli's door for her and held it while she used the runners on his truck to get to her seat. She even did that with a delicate femininity that had Spur wanting to put his hand on the small of her back or her waist to steady her.

He managed to keep his hands to himself, because that touch-barrier hadn't been broken yet. She'd flipped his tie slightly, but there'd been no skin-to-skin contact. Spur closed the door and swallowed, his mind racing ahead through that night. He'd hold her hand. Laugh with her. Put his arm around her...

Maybe, he sternly told himself as he went around to the driver's seat. *So much a maybe.*

If he did all that, he'd be playing his real hand. This was supposed to be a friendly date where they got to know one another so they could pull the wool over someone's eyes. *Friendly,* he reminded himself.

Annoyed with himself for having to remind himself of what was really happening here, and the fact that he'd used a sheep metaphor in that reminder, he got behind the wheel and looked at Olli. "Is Six Stars okay?"

She looked at him, excitement in her eyes. "Spur Chappell, do you dance?"

A chuckle flowed from his mouth as easily as breathing. Everything about being with Olli was easy, and he couldn't believe he'd missed that too. He also really liked his full name in her soft, Southern drawl.

"Yes, ma'am," he said, ducking his head and starting the truck. "My momma taught all of us boys. Said it was a life lesson a man ought to be able to do."

"Well, I'll be," Olli said with a smile. "I like your mother more already. Six Stars is great." She laughed, and Spur liked the sound of that too. Surely there would be something about Olli he wouldn't like, and he thought of Katie as he pulled around the circle drive in front of Olli's house.

"She's a character, my mother," Spur said, his mind working overtime. "Listen, uh, I just found out about a family picnic this weekend. I was thinking..." He couldn't quite finish, because he'd been thinking so dang much that his thoughts had started to cross. He went to the end of her driveway and turned toward the highway that led into town.

They lived in a sprawling, small town in the Lexington hills, and Spur had loved growing up in Horse Country, specifically Dreamsville. The town was founded by the three Dreams brothers, and there were descendants of the family still living there.

Spur wasn't particularly romantic, but he felt like dreams really did come true in Dreamsville, and while he traveled somewhat for his job, he always loved coming back home.

He reached to adjust the volume on the radio, one of the classic Garth Brooks songs coming on. No sooner had he pulled his hand back than Olli stretched out and lowered the volume again. "You were thinking what?" she asked, peering at him more closely now.

Spur shifted in his seat as he looked past her to see if there was any oncoming traffic. "What did I say?"

"You said you found out about a family picnic this weekend, and you were thinking—dot, dot, dot."

He liked that she hadn't just let him off the hook. At the same time, that blasted hook had lodged in his throat, and he couldn't spit out the words. He made the turn and told himself to stop acting like he was twenty years old. He was most decidedly *not* twenty, and he could just say what was on his mind.

"I thought we should go," he said.

"Together?" Olli asked.

Spur hated the surprise in her voice. He hated it so much that he frowned at her. "We'll have all this week to get to know each other. Get our story straight. Your guy is coming in a couple of weeks, right?" He barely glanced at her, though this long stretch of road didn't require much attention from him.

"Yes," she said.

Spur shrugged, hoping to play this off as nothing. If she'd reacted differently, he might be spilling his guts right now. "Well, my mother is extraordinarily good at seeing things she shouldn't. I figured the picnic might be a great dry run for us. You know, a halfway point, to see if we can come off as a convincing, committed couple."

He looked out his window as the Dixon Ranch came up on his left. They ran an amazing operation too, and Spur had a lot of respect for Bethany Dixon and all she'd done since her husband's death two or three years ago. Spur had used the idea of her and her ranch many times to keep his cool about things happening—or not happening—at the Bluegrass Ranch. He told himself that if she could produce champion horses with just herself and a half-dozen cowboys, he certainly could with just himself and his seven brothers.

They had a lot more help than that at Bluegrass, but it was also ten times the size of Dixon.

"A trial run," Olli mused, and Spur pulled himself back to the present. "It's not a terrible idea."

"Thanks," he said dryly.

Olli giggled, and though he knew she was in her forties, he wasn't sure which number came after that initial four. "I remember Ginny Winters decorating your whole place with black balloons and streamers and all that a few years ago," he said. "I can't recall exactly how many."

"Mister Chappell, are you asking me how old I am?"

"Yes, ma'am," he said. "I think a serious boyfriend would know that about his serious girlfriend."

"Ginny draped my garage door and my front door in black plastic," Olli said, fondness replacing the flirtatiousness in her voice. "It was four years ago. I'm forty-four."

"Ah, Cayden's age." He wondered why she didn't just ask him to be her stand-in arm candy. He decided to simply ask. "Why didn't you ask him to play this part?"

"Can you handle the truth?"

He looked at her, finding her green eyes dancing with mischief. She was very good at the flirtation game, and Spur needed to up his. "I sure can," he said.

"I thought about asking Cayden. He was my first choice."

"Ouch," Spur said, adding a chuckle to the word so his real wounded feelings wouldn't show. Subconsciously, his fingers strangled the steering wheel, and he had to mentally coach himself to release them.

"Then you showed up on that pretty bay, saved me from certain death-by-sheep-trampling, and swept me off my feet."

Spur burst out laughing, glad when Olli did too. Everything lightened then, and he actually thought he could reach across the distance between them and take her hand in his. He did not, but he thought he could. "Certain death-by-sheep-trampling," he repeated, still laughing between the words. "Sheep are harmless, Olli."

"Not when they're coming straight at you," she said. "And

you're shoeless and can't run anyway. I thought the last sound I'd hear was that of a bunch of herding dogs barking, as sheep foot after sheep foot trampled the life out of me."

"Okay, first, sheep have *hooves*," he said, starting up another round of laughter.

Olli joined him again, and Spur laughed until her hand touched his and took it from the steering wheel. His voice muted then, and all he could do was marvel at the soft yet insistent tug of her touch as she pulled his hand closer to her and twined their fingers together.

"What's second?" she asked, but Spur had no idea what they'd been talking about. He looked at her, the mood in the cab much different now that she'd touched him.

"You have soft skin," he blurted out, immediately wanting to shove something in his mouth that would prevent him from speaking again.

She smiled, though. "Thanks, Spur." She drew in an audible breath, and Spur felt like he needed to take one too. "So I'm forty-four. Ginny Winters is my best friend. You're forty...six, I think?"

He nodded, and she continued with, "And you own and operate the biggest and best horse breeding ranch in northern Kentucky."

He laughed and shook his head. "I wish, but it's a nice statement."

"You're not the biggest and best?"

"Oh, we're the best," he said. "Just not the biggest."

"Your place is *huge*," she said.

"I'm glad you think so," he said, though he supposed Bluegrass Ranch was bigger than other breeding ranches. They did more, that was all. They stabled horses too, and trainers came to work their owner's horses. Their track was open seven days a week, and Trey, the third oldest brother, managed that entire branch of Bluegrass.

"We're only about six hundred acres," he said. "There are stables and breeding facilities three times that big around Horse Country."

"But you *are* the best," she said in that flirtatious tone that got Spur's pulse pounding.

"Yes, ma'am."

"So Kentucky-Southern proper, too," she said. "You just might win my heart for real, Spur Chappell."

He looked at her again, not even caring if he drove right off the road. "What does it take to do that?" he asked.

She met his gaze, her eyebrows going up. "I don't know."

"You've never been married?" he asked.

"No, sir."

"You've dated though."

"Sure," she said, finally breaking their connection and looking out her window instead of at him. "I was engaged once."

He wanted to know more about that, and he squeezed her hand to indicate as much.

"You were married," she said instead.

"Yes," he said. "Her name was Katie. We were together five years. Been divorced for eight now."

Olli nodded, the mood all over the place and they hadn't even made it to Six Stars yet. The restaurant-slash-dance-hall wouldn't be terribly crowded on a Monday night, but it was always noisy. He second-guessed his choice for dinner, because they needed time to talk. He'd wanted to take her dancing though, because he knew if he did, he'd be able to hold her in his arms.

"I was engaged to a man named Hazard. Well, his real name was Sherman, but everyone called him Hazard." She delivered an audible sigh. "I should've known from just the name that he'd be trouble for me."

"You never did get married?"

"He called it off the morning before our wedding day."

Spur whistled in a way that conveyed his disbelief and disgust. "Olli, I'm sorry."

"I wish I could whistle like that," she said.

Spur made the final turn and Six Stars appeared up ahead. "You can't whistle?"

She puckered her lips and pushed air through them, barely making any sound at all. "Does that count?" She grinned at him with plenty of that sparkle, and Spur laughed for the third time in the short twenty-minute drive.

"No, ma'am," he said. "That does not count. That's really the best you can do?"

"Some of us aren't perfect at everything," she teased, and Spur shook his head. He wasn't either, that was for sure.

"Can you at least dance?" he asked, finding and taking a parking space in the main lot. Six Stars had two overflow lots, but his prediction about the Monday night crowd was right. He'd attended the dancehall on the weekend before, and every spot would be filled then.

"Of course I can dance, Mister," she said. "I took lessons from old Ingrid herself."

"Stay," he said, killing the engine and hopping out of the cab. He hurried around to her side and opened the door for her.

"I'm not a dog, you know," she said, grinning at him as she slid out of his truck. Her skirt hitched higher on her legs, and Olli quickly pulled it down once she'd landed on her feet. She wore a bright blue pair of heels Spur hadn't noticed at the house, but now that he'd seen them, he couldn't look away. "You like my shoes?" she asked, cocking one ankle.

"Yes, ma'am," he said, his voice coming out dry and rusted. He looked at her, a heated charge flowing between them. She had to feel that. He couldn't be the only one getting scorched right now. "I like them. Very sexy."

Olli's face split into a smile, and Spur reached out and tucked her hair behind her ear. Time froze for a moment, and thankfully, Spur's thoughts did too. Then, everything rushed forward again, and he was left wondering how much truth that simple gesture had told her.

She stepped out of the doorway and linked her arm through his. "You know what, Spur? No one's called me sexy for a while, and I think you just earned yourself a lot of bonus points."

"Is that right?" He closed the door quickly, and they started toward the restaurant's entrance. "What can a man do with his bonus points?"

Olli tipped her head back and laughed, the sound spilling into the sky and striking Spur right in the heart. "Nothing, silly. They're not even real." She grinned up at him, and Spur couldn't help grinning right on back down.

"Fine," he said. "But you shouldn't give points if they don't mean anything." He opened the door for her, sure he'd mess something up in the next couple of weeks, and it would be nice if he could use some of his accumulated bonus points to get back in her good graces. He determined he'd simply use them anyway, because he knew Olli well enough to know she'd like that game.

"Oh," Olli said, releasing his arm and clapping her hands a couple of times. She looked at him, pure delight brightening her whole face. "It's waltz night. I *love* the waltz."

"Perfect," Spur said, holding up two fingers for the hostess. He stepped closer to her and said, "Somewhere a little quieter for dinner, if you can."

"Sure," she drawled with a smile. As she led them past the dance floor, Spur had never been more grateful for his mother and her insane drive to teach all eight of her boys how to dance —including the waltz.

CHAPTER 5

"Okay," Olli said, ready to get down to business. The drive to Six Stars had been amazing, and Olli wondered what about Spur had scared her in the past. He was nothing but pure Southern gentleman and extreme good looks. Maybe that was exactly what had intimidated her.

"Okay," he said back, and she realized she'd fallen into staring into those dark, dreamy eyes and losing time.

She cleared her throat. "Rapid-fire time. Short questions. Short answers. Favorites. Middle names. All the stuff we should know about each other. Little things."

"So not the long, detailed stories of our painful break-ups," he said with a smile.

Olli smiled too and shook her head. "Definitely not that." There'd be more time for that, she was sure. She hoped. She couldn't believe she'd been so bold as to coax his hand away from the steering wheel. He'd been clenching it so tightly, and something inside her just wanted him to relax.

He had too, and she honestly couldn't remember ever hearing Spur Chappell laugh before. He'd held her hand the whole way to town too, and Olli couldn't help it if she was a more touchy-feely type of woman. She *loved* hanging on a handsome man's arm, and she'd forgotten just how much.

"I'll start," she said, gathering her hair and putting it over her shoulders as if preparing for battle. "Siblings?"

"Seven brothers. You?"

"Just the two. One brother. One sister. Both younger than me. Both married with children." She didn't mean to deliver those facts with any bitterness at all, but it had been there, bright and hot on her tongue.

If Spur heard it, he didn't indicate. "I'm the oldest too," he said. "A couple of my brothers are dating people right now, but none of us are married."

"But you have been."

"Yes."

"Anyone else?"

"Ian, for about half a year," Spur said. "Blaine was engaged once. Trey too."

Olli nodded. She wanted those stories for sure, just not right now. "Favorite food, go."

"French fries. No, wait, red licorice. Wait." He grinned. "French fries."

She grinned at him. He was so easy to talk to, and she couldn't believe she'd never seen that before.

"What do you do in your spare time?" he asked.

"I don't have spare time. Do you?"

"Not much, but I do like to go horseback riding every chance I get, and believe it or not, I like to—" He cleared his throat in a semi-aggressive, grinding kind of way. "I like to knit while I watch a show in the evening, right before bed."

Olli blinked, sure she'd heard him wrong. "Okay, wait." She held up both hands and leaned back in the booth. The picture in her mind was just too hilarious. "I'm seeing you sitting up in bed, like, I don't know. The Big Bad Wolf or something. Knitting in the near darkness with the flickering TV on. Is that what you're telling me?"

Spur looked mildly horrified. "The Big Bad Wolf?"

"You know, after he's swallowed the granny in the story. He's wearing that nightgown and that little flowered cap." Her grin felt like it would crack her face in half. "She—he—knits while he waits for Little Red Riding Hood to show up."

"No," Spur practically barked. "There is no nightgown, and no little flowered cap. I watch this horse rescue operation show, and I just need something to keep my hands busy."

"What do you make?" she asked.

"Trivets," he said, and Olli barely contained her laughter. "Hats. Pot holders. I started a blanket once, but I don't have the attention span for that."

"So something you can make in an evening."

"How long do you think it takes to knit a hat?" he asked.

"I have no idea, Spur," she teased. "I don't knit before bed."

"Okay," he said, leaning back too. "I shouldn't have told you that. Next question."

"Spur—"

"How long have you been making perfume?" he asked, his dark eyes flashing dangerously now.

"Seven years," she said.

"What did you do before that?"

"Led tours at horse farms."

"Favorite color?"

"Yellow." Olli suddenly hated the game, because Spur was just firing things off now. There was nothing fun or flirty about it, and Olli regretted that she'd taken her teasing too far.

He opened his mouth to shoot something else at her, but she held up her hand and he paused.

"I'm sorry," she said as sincerely as she could. "I think it's great you found something to keep your hands busy while you relax in the evening."

He lowered his chin just two inches, but it was enough to conceal his eyes beneath the brim of that very sexy cowboy hat. How men did that—lowered their heads the exact right amount to hide only what they wanted to hide—she didn't know. They must practice in front of a mirror every dang day.

"Is Spur your real name?"

"Yes, ma'am."

Olli smiled at the softness in his voice, though he still hadn't lifted his head again. "Do you like fishing?"

"Not particularly."

She took a moment to take a breath. "Favorite color?"

"Black. Dark blue." He looked up then, something powerful and yet vulnerable passing between them. She extended her hand across the table, only intending to go halfway. He met her in the middle and squeezed her hand.

"I am sorry about teasing you about the knitting," she said.

"It's fine," he said. "You did use up some of the bonus points you earned when you called my cowboy casual necktie sexy, though." His eyes sparkled now, all of their previous darkness gone. "Just so you know."

Olli blinked at him, burst out laughing, and began bargaining with herself about how far she could take this fake relationship.

Maybe it's not fake at all, she thought, but she didn't dare bring that up during the rest of their getting-to-know-you game.

* * *

The next morning, Olli woke with a happiness hangover. She stayed under the covers and kept her eyes closed, reliving one of the best nights of her life. Spur had lightened up after her apology, and they'd had a great evening together.

The man could *dance*, and Olli wanted to see him again immediately. They'd made no further plans to get together, and she rolled over and picked up her phone, intending to change that.

As she'd stood in Spur's arms last night, laughing and dancing, she'd caught a whiff of his cologne. The man smelled amazing, and she needed to know what brand of cologne he wore. She also needed him to step into her world for a moment and help her find the best male scents for her new line of men's products.

She started five different texts, each of them getting erased. She didn't want to be long-winded, as Spur had said he didn't have spare time. She seized onto the knitting, a smile forming on her face.

Wondered if you'd like to keep your hands busy at my perfumery tonight? I'd love your help with a line of men's products I'm developing. My nose is decidedly female, and I need some Y-chromosomal input.

Before she could doubt herself for the sixth time, she sent the hopefully fun, flirty message across the acres between their two houses.

She sat up and stretched, deciding she better get out of bed before she fell back asleep. She had plenty to do at the perfumery that day, especially if tall, dreamy Spur was going to be there that night.

Panic's grip tightened around her lungs. "Why did you invite him to the perfumery?" She rolled her eyes at herself as she stood. If her house could be called a mess, the perfumery should probably be deemed a natural disaster area. There was no way she could spruce it up before that evening, even if she went straight there now and cleaned all day.

"It's fine," she muttered to herself when her phone stayed silent. "He won't come anyway. He's your *fake* boyfriend, Olli. Not your real one."

She walked into the bathroom, nearly tripping over Witcher. "Oh," she said to the black cat as she steadied herself with a hand against the doorjamb. "You must be out of food."

The cat never came out of hiding except for when he was out of food. Even when Olli sat on the couch at night, the TV blaring in front of her, Witcher stayed hidden. She'd had him for a few years now, and she'd gotten him from the animal shelter to have as a companion. She saw him less than she saw her own shadow, and that honestly would've been a better companion than the cat.

She detoured into the kitchen to get his bowl. She put it on the plastic mat by the back door, but Witcher always pawed it under the kitchen table to actually eat. She found his back-story immensely interesting, and she wished he could talk to her and tell her why he did what he did.

Cats couldn't talk to humans, though, so Olli used the long broomstick to poke the empty bowl out from under-neath the table. Witcher meowed as she washed it with hot, soapy water, dried it, and filled it with more cat chow.

She put it on the plastic mat, and Witcher immediately began to swat at it. "You can just eat it right there," Olli said. "I won't even watch." She bent to pick up his water bowl, and got that cleaned and refilled too.

She'd just set it down when the buzzing sound of a weed-whacker or lawn mower met her ears.

Turning toward the front door, Olli's surprise doubled. Who was at her house, doing yard work? Despite still wearing her pajamas, she crossed the dining room and kitchen and into the living room, her goal the front door.

She opened it only a couple of inches, hoping she'd just been mistaken. The buzzing grew louder, because someone was definitely here doing yard work.

Olli stepped out onto the front porch and walked to the top of the steps. A man stood out in the ruined bed of four o'clocks, using an electric pair of handheld trimmers to clean up the ruined plants.

The morning light shone off his dark cowboy hat, and Olli distinctly knew the feel and width of those shoulders. She knew the strength in Spur's large hands, and her heart started fluttering in a most unnatural way.

Spur continued to work, and Olli continued to watch him. He'd come to do the work himself instead of sending one of the men who worked at Bluegrass Ranch. He could've sent anyone, and yet...

Warmth filled Olli, and she leaned against the pillar on her porch, wondering if this fake relationship with Spur could become real. She'd sensed something in him last night, but it had been hard to put into words. She wasn't even sure she believed the spark of attraction she'd seen in his eyes. It had only lasted for a moment anyway.

Spur turned toward her, and Olli straightened, her pulse pouncing now. *Too late*, she thought as Spur killed the trimmer and lifted his hand in a wave. He'd seen her.

Worse, he started walking toward her. All Olli could think about was how bad her breath must smell, and how disheveled her hair usually was in the morning. She hadn't showered or caffeinated, and the most handsome, kind, and helpful man on the planet was walking straight toward her.

"Morning," Spur said pleasantly. He looked all properly put together in a pair of blue jeans, his work cowboy boots, and a white, blue, and orange checkered shirt.

"Good morning," she said.

"I didn't wake you with the clippers, did I?" His eyes swept down to her feet and back to her eyes.

Olli shifted, though she didn't find any judgment in his gaze. It seemed like a spark rested in his eyes, and Olli marveled at that for a moment. Could that be a spark of attraction?

"No," she managed to say. "Did you want some coffee?" She indicated the house behind her, feeling self-conscious about her clothing and the state of everything she hadn't brushed, cleaned, or washed yet. "I was just about to put some on."

"Sure," he said easily. He blinked and the spark was gone. Olli had probably imagined it.

Of course you did, she told herself as she turned around and went back inside. The moment she did, she paused, realizing her mistake. She should not have invited him inside her home. She took a big breath, trying to decide what to do. Her nose filled with the scent of something she'd made for dinner long ago, and she really needed to hire a maid service to help her get caught up on her housekeeping.

She turned around and nearly slammed into the very solid body of Spur. "I changed my mind. Let's go out for coffee."

"We're already in," he said, his hand sliding down from her shoulder to her elbow as he backed up a step.

Time slowed down until it stopped, and Olli couldn't look away from Spur's face. A very real attraction to him bubbled within her, and she was sure it showed on her face. That was bad news. The good news was that Spur had the same fiery interest resting in his eyes, and suddenly Olli knew her fake boyfriend had feelings for her too.

Her stomach swooped. He removed his hand from her elbow. She cleared her throat. "I'm not a very good housekeeper," she said, ducking her head. "I'm embarrassed."

"It's fine," Spur said. "At our place, Blaine brews the coffee, because when I do it, everyone complains about how bitter it is."

She looked up at him, finding a smile on that mouth. She wanted to kiss that mouth so badly, and her whole body flushed.

"Everyone has something they're not great at," he said. "We probably should've talked about that last night." He sidestepped her and went a few more paces into the house before he stopped, obviously surveying it. "It's not bad, Olli, honestly."

"Okay," she said, though she didn't believe him. She went into the kitchen, trying not to see all the things she hadn't put away yet. The shoes, the mail, and the water bottles. The recyclable grocery bags, the empty boxes of ice cream bars.

Humiliation filled her, but instead of getting out a garbage bag and cleaning up, she filled the coffee pot with water. "What else aren't you good at?" she asked.

Spur settled at her bar, gently nudging an unopened box that likely contained vials out of the way. "Oh, let's see." He exhaled for a few seconds. "My mother would say I'm terrible at reading a room. I've had to work really hard to win over customers and clients over the years." He smiled at her, and if he knew how devastatingly handsome it made him, he didn't show it. "My brothers would say I'm bad at keeping my opinions to myself, and-or admitting I'm wrong."

Olli returned the smile. "I'm not great at admitting it when I'm wrong either." She measured out the coffee and set it to brew. "There's the housekeeping." She picked up the bottle of water she'd gotten out last night after Spur had dropped her off. "I guess I just don't have the patience for it."

"What else?" he asked. "I gave you three."

"Dressing myself," Olli said, turning to get mugs out of the cupboard.

"Excuse me?" Spur asked, a laugh in the two words. It came out of his mouth a moment later. "Did you say dressing yourself? Who dresses you?"

Olli turned back to him and put the mugs on the counter. "Not like that," she said, giggling a little with him. "I just meant, when I'm getting ready for something important, I never know what to wear. What I think is cute and fashionable, usually isn't."

Spur nodded and said, "Keep going."

"Like, last night for example. I wanted to look amazing, and I picked out these ankle boots. Ginny told me I couldn't even be buried in them."

His eyes blazed at her, and Olli really wanted to get burned. "Ginny helps you."

"Yes," Olli said. "She's great with fashion and knowing how to tuck, and what accessories to use. Which colors go with which. She put me in a pair of pale pink shorts once, and then made me wear this pumpkin-orange blouse with it. I didn't think it looked good *at all*, but I got a ton of compliments at the Harvest Fest, and I sold out of all of my seasonal candles by lunch." Olli shook her head just thinking about it. "I never go anywhere or do anything important without Ginny's fashion help."

Spur nodded, his eyes never leaving hers. "You said she dressed you last night?"

"Yes."

They looked at one another, and Olli realized what she'd just said and how much she'd just given away. "I mean—"

The coffee pot started to percolate, and she spun toward it. She didn't have anything to attend to, though. She simply stared as the first drops of coffee dripped into the pot. She might as well have told him she'd been thinking about him since the moment she'd awakened that morning, and that she'd started fantasizing about him as her real boyfriend and not fake filler for an investor.

She reached into the cupboard beside the stove for sugar and ignored the scraping of the barstool as Spur stood. He'd probably leave now, because he wasn't interested in her. He'd been willing to do her a favor, but now that he knew she had real feelings for him—real feelings she hadn't even known about—he'd tell her to find someone else to be her arm candy.

She set the sugar bowl on the counter beside the coffee maker and opened the fridge to get the cream.

"Olli," Spur said, and it was downright criminal how soft he'd said her name. If he did it again, she might just swoon into the counter behind her.

She looked up, the pint of cream in her hand.

"Last night was important to me too," he said. She'd never

heard him speak with such tenderness. Not to her, not to anyone.

Their eyes met as he lifted his gaze to hers, and Olli wasn't sure if she swooned or an earthquake hit Kentucky. She did stumble into the counter behind her, glad it was there to keep her from falling.

Spur held up his phone. "My brother just texted about a horse I have to attend to, so I'll take a rain check on the coffee."

"Okay," she said, still not sure what he meant by *last night was important to me too.*

"I'd love to come by the perfumery tonight. What time?"

Olli shrugged and said, "Whenever. Just come over here, and I'll take you."

"Say seven-thirty?" he asked.

"Sure."

"Okay," he said, stepping toward her. Actually toward her. He leaned down and brushed his lips along her hairline. "See you then."

He walked toward the front door, but Olli didn't dare turn and watch him, just in case this was a dream and she woke up when she moved.

When the door clicked closed, time flowed again. Olli looked around and felt the cold pint of cream in her hand and smelled the hot coffee as it continued to drip.

"That wasn't a dream," she whispered to herself, one hand reaching up to touch the tingling, heated spot on her forehead where Spur had kissed her.

CHAPTER 6

S pur hadn't told any of his brothers about his date with Olli the night before. Yet somehow, when he walked into the sick bay after Blaine's text, his brother's first question was, "Did I take you from Olli?"

Cayden and Trey both looked at him too, and Spur quickly said, "What's wrong with Glory?"

Leroy had his stethoscope on, and the fact that the vet was here already meant Blaine hadn't texted Spur right away.

"She's fine," Leroy said, smiling. "Her heart rate is normal, and her eyes are clear."

Fine was not what Spur wanted. All For Glory could fetch them almost a million dollars, and every little hiccup worried him.

"Why did they call you?" he asked, wanting to hear it from the vet and not his brothers. Three of them stood there—the three most tied to the horse care and operations at Bluegrass Ranch.

Blaine oversaw the health of all of their animals, the horses included. Trey managed the track, the trainers, and the housing for the horses. Cayden did all the scheduling for trainers, individual horses, and the buying and selling the ranch participated in.

Spur scanned the lot of them and looked back at Leroy as he started to talk. "Blaine said she took a moment to get up this morning," Leroy said.

"She was just slow," Blaine said.

"I was just walking by," Cayden said. "So I came in."

"I just saw Leroy when he arrived," Trey added. "That's why I'm here."

"Y'all are terrible liars," Spur growled. "I know when you start spitting out 'just this' and 'just that.'" He glared at the three of them. "What's wrong with Glory?" he asked again.

Blaine looked at Leroy and back to Spur, and if he didn't start talking, Spur wasn't sure what he'd do, but it wouldn't be pretty. "She stumbled this morning, Spur," he said, his voice even and his mouth settling into a straight line afterward.

"Stumbled? Where?"

"Coming out of the stall," Blaine said. "For no reason. There was nothing there. She went down to her front knees, and I called Leroy to see what was going on."

Spur stepped over to the pretty gray horse that looked like she'd been sprayed with pepper. He loved her, and not just for the money she could bring to the ranch. Spur had plenty of money, though the drive to make more and keep the ranch thriving also ran hotly through him. "What's goin' on,

Glory?" he asked the horse, using the same soft voice he'd used when speaking to Olli.

His face heated, but not because his brothers had caught him talking to another horse. He couldn't believe he'd told Olli last night was important to him too. It had been, though, and Spur was far too old to play games with a woman.

He'd been pleased as punch when Olli had said she called Ginny to dress her whenever she had something important to look nice for. He'd felt important, and he'd seen Olli's feelings in her eyes while they stood in front of the fridge, her clutching that carton of cream like it alone could save her.

A smile touched his mouth. He'd get to see her that night, and maybe they could have a real conversation about a real relationship.

Don't go too fast, cowboy, he told himself, pulling on the reins attached to his heart. He knew what bursting out of the gate looked like and felt like, and the horse would be dead before it got to the first turn on the track.

It was always better to start slow, work up to a race pace, and finish strong.

Stop thinking about women in terms of horse racing, he told himself next, glad when Leroy spoke again. Then Spur wouldn't have to keep talking to himself or horses.

"I'd like to monitor her for a few days. Like I said, her eyes are clear and her heart rate is normal. I don't see anything that would indicate a problem or that would cause her to stumble."

"Can she run?" Spur asked.

"I'd like to observe a light training session," Leroy said.

"I'll get Kara," Cayden said, stepping away.

Spur stayed close to Glory and ignored his brothers as they all moved to the practice track to watch Glory do an easy training day. Once Kara had her moving around the track at a walk, Spur relaxed. He could spot a good horse from a mile away, and Glory was amazing. Her legs looked too long for her body, which was exactly what he wanted in a good racing horse. She loved to run, and she kept trying to pick up the pace though Kara held her back.

"She looks good," Trey said, and he had an eye for horses too. They all did, as horse breeding and racing had been in their blood for generations and generations.

Spur put his right foot up on the bottom rung and let his hands hang over the top one. Glory rounded the curve in the track, and he lost sight of her.

"I can watch her," Blaine said. "You get back to Olli."

"What's with you and Olli?" Cayden asked before Spur could say he didn't need to get back to Olli.

"Nothing's with us," Spur said, not quite sure if their relationship was secret or not. He assumed it wasn't, but he also wasn't sure if he should keep that it was fake under wraps.

It's not fake, he told himself. His feelings for her were very, very real, and he'd kissed her before he'd left her standing in her kitchen. His foot on the bottom rung twitched, and a healthy shot of embarrassment filled him. He'd *kissed* her. What had he been thinking?

He'd blown *fake* right out of the water with that blasted kiss.

Olli hadn't said anything to him though, and Spur *had* seen that glint of attraction in her eyes.

"You're not a great liar either," Blaine said. "Just so you know."

Spur physically flinched, but he didn't know what else to say. He didn't want to lie to his brothers, all of whom could've passed for him on a semi-dark night. All the Chappell brothers stood over six feet tall, all wore cowboy hats and boots and jeans. They all had the scent of horses clinging to them all the time, and they all woke with the sun and worked until they couldn't stand for another moment.

He loved his brothers powerfully, but he didn't owe them any explanations.

"Are you dating her?" Trey asked, his eyes still out on the track, waiting for Glory to round the right bend.

"Can you guys not hound me about this?" Spur asked, keeping his gaze beyond the conversation too. "She's just a friend I was helping out."

"I just think it's noteworthy," Trey said, his voice pitching up. "If you're dating Olivia Hudson, that's all."

"Why would that be noteworthy?" Spur asked.

"Uh, hello?" Blaine said. "How about because you haven't dated in forever, and just last week you said you were, and I quote, 'never going to get married again'."

Spur had said that, and a sting of humiliation added to the embarrassment still swirling through him.

"Things change," Cayden said. "Spur does like to help his neighbors and friends out."

"Exactly," Spur said. "So leave me alone."

"When are you going to see her again?" Trey asked.

"Tonight," Spur said without thinking.

Silence descended upon them, and Spur pressed his eyes closed when he realized what he'd just admitted to.

Thankfully, Blaine's phone rang, and he said, "Oh, it's Tam. I have to take this." He stepped away, his voice cheerful and bright when he said hello to his friend. Spur couldn't help thinking that Blaine and Tam were best friends and yet no one was accusing him of dating the woman.

Glory came around the bend, and Kara eased her into a trot.

"She looks good," Trey said, standing up on the bottom rung now. "No hitches, no twitching movement, nothing."

Spur had to agree, and he hoped and prayed that her stumble that morning had just been a fluke. "Let's have Leroy watch her anyway," Spur said as Blaine rejoined them and Glory rounded the left bend again. "Okay, Blaine? I want her monitored for the next five days, round the clock."

"Around the clock?" Blaine shook his head, his expression falling. "You're killing me, Spur."

"Get Tam to come sit with her," Spur said. "She loves doing that." He smiled at Blaine and started to walk away. "I have to get back to work. Keep me informed if anything comes up."

"Have fun with Olli tonight," Cayden called, and the three of them twittered behind him.

Spur just kept walking, because he wanted to have fun with Olli that night. As an added measure, he threw up a prayer that they would have fun that night. And maybe he could kiss her again, this time closer to her mouth.

* * *

Spur looped the tie around his neck and then took it off again. Three times, he'd done that, and he still couldn't decide if he should wear it or not.

"Not," he said, tossing it into the sink in front of him. "You're not taking her to dinner. She's going to use you as a tester for her men's colognes." He scanned himself in the bathroom mirror. He was definitely trying too hard with the slacks.

He stripped them off and stepped into a pair of clean jeans. "Better," he muttered. He'd changed his shirt, and he wondered if that was trying too hard too. He reasoned that any man would come in from a long day of working and shower, thus requiring a change of clothes.

Would a man just sniffing colognes need to wear the cowboy hat he wore to church? Or the boots that had never licked up dust on the ranch?

He had no idea, and he didn't have someone like Ginny to call and ask. He thought of Blaine, who had dated much more often than Spur ever had...

He pulled out his phone and sent a quick text. Two minutes later, he was still standing in the bathroom, trying to make impossible decisions, when his brother knocked and came into the room.

"Spur?"

"In the bathroom," he called, and Blaine appeared in the doorway several seconds later.

Their eyes met in the mirror, and Spur was going to have to admit some things out loud. "I like Olivia Hudson," he blurted. "She asked me to be her fake boyfriend for an investor she has to impress in a couple of weeks, and I suggested we go out to get to know one another and get our story straight."

Blaine folded his arms, his face a perfect mask of I-knew-it. "You want to take fake to feasible."

"Yes," Spur admitted. "Can you tell by what I'm wearing?" He turned toward Blaine. "I don't want to be ultra-obvious."

"Why not?" Blaine asked, scanning Spur from head to toe. "What do you have to hide?"

"I don't know," Spur said. "Is that what people do now? Just come out and say, 'I like you and I don't want this to be fake'?"

"I don't know about people, Spur," Blaine said. "You've never been normal people."

"I don't know if that's a compliment or not." He pointed to the cowboy hat on the counter. "If I wear that, am I being too obvious?"

"No," Blaine said. "You don't want to wear a smelly, sweaty hat you've been working in all day."

"Okay." Spur settled the hat he wore to church on his head. "Last night, I wore new boots. Tonight?" He looked at Blaine. "We're just going to her perfumery. She wants me to help her with the men's line she's developing."

"Uh huh," Blaine said. "I'm sure she does."

"She does," Spur said. "That's what she said."

"Is there any indication this woman likes you too? That it might not be fake for her either?"

"I don't—maybe?" Spur hated guessing, but he *had* been out of the dating arena for a while, and he wasn't exactly sure what he'd seen in Olli's gaze. "Read her text. You tell me." He indicated the phone on the counter, second-and-third-guessing everything he'd thought he'd seen in her expression that morning. "I'm going to get the new boots. Might as well."

He left Blaine in the bathroom and went into the closet to get the boots. He took them to the bed and sat down to pull them on.

"I think it's a good call with the clean boots," Blaine said. "This text is super flirty, Spur."

"Is it?"

"Definitely." Blaine handed him his phone. "Maybe you should take flowers too, and just lead with the 'I like you' statement."

Spur read Olli's text again. He hadn't answered, because he'd read it while he sat at her kitchen counter, her back to him after he'd basically called her out for saying their date last night was important to her. She'd said she wanted to look amazing... maybe this text *was* super flirty.

"We should ask Duke," Spur said. "He'd know."

"*I* know," Blaine said. "Ask him if you want, but if you think you were annoyed when Trey, Cayden, and I were teasing you, you haven't seen anything yet."

"You're right," Spur murmured. He couldn't involve Duke, even if he was thirteen years younger than Spur and right on the cusp of the cool single adult culture. Spur wasn't interested in being cool.

"Hey," Blaine said, and Spur looked away from his phone. Blaine was the middle brother, and Spur had always gotten along really well with him. Right now, he wore an intense look in his eyes, which weren't quite as dark as Spur's.

"You like her," he said gently. "So what? It's normal to like a woman."

"It's *Olli*," Spur said.

"So what?"

"She's our next-door neighbor," Spur said. "I don't know. I just...I've never admitted that I liked her for more than that."

"Maybe it's time to admit it."

"I just did," Spur said.

"To her," Blaine said.

That would be much harder, Spur knew. He nodded anyway and said, "I have to get going. I said I'd be there at seven-thirty." He glanced at his knitting basket on the nightstand and instinctively reached for one of the trivets he'd finished a few nights ago.

He pulled up to Olli's house several minutes later, the blue and white trivet mocking him now. At the same time, he wanted to share it with her. He grabbed it before he could get too deep inside his thoughts and headed for the front door.

He'd stood here last night and rung this same doorbell. It was just as nerve-racking tonight, listening to the chimes ring through the house on the other side of the door. Olli's footsteps came closer; the door opened.

She stood there wearing a pair of skin-tight black jeans and a blouse the color of pink lemonade. He wanted to scoop her right into his arms and breathe in her tantalizing scent. Instead, he thrust the trivet toward her. "I brought you this," he said, hating himself a little more with every word.

Olli took it from him, a smile spreading across her face. "Thank you, Spur." She moved back a couple of steps. "Come in for a sec. I have to find my shoes."

He noticed her bare feet then, and he sure did like the casualness of her. Gone was her embarrassment from that morning, when she'd also been shoeless. Of course, she'd also been in her pajamas and worried about what he'd think of her messy house.

He didn't mind much, because his house had been utter chaos growing up. Most of the time, it still was. He lived with three of his brothers, while the other four lived in a second property on the north side of the ranch. When he'd been married to Katie, the two of them had lived in a house on the outskirts of Dreamsville, a short six-minute drive to the ranch and stables.

Spur closed the door behind him as Olli put the trivet on the kitchen counter. It had been cleared of all the stuff he'd seen there that morning, and he looked around at the house. "You cleaned up," he said.

"I called a maid service," she said over her shoulder. "Don't be impressed."

He watched her hips swing as she left him in the living area and went down the hall, and he was definitely impressed. He cleared his throat, wishing he wasn't quite so hormonal, and glanced around again.

Olli had pictures of her family on the table near the front door. He eased further into the house and found watercolor paintings on the walls in the living room, tasteful furniture he hadn't noticed that morning because he'd been so focused on Olli, and scented candles on every available surface.

He picked up the one nearest to him and examined the label. *Midnight Messenger* it read, and it promised Good News, Sweet Dreams, and A Hopeful Future in the deep blue candle wax.

Below those words sat the scents of pineapple, lavender, and toasted sugar. He lifted the candle to his nose, noting it had not been lit before, and took a deep breath in. "That is nice," he said, replacing the candle on the shelf.

He couldn't even imagine coming up with unique names for candles, and then naming scents things like *Good News*.

He marveled at Olli's creativity and reached for the next candle. This one was bright white, and it was called *Get Your Man*. Spur blinked, wondering what a woman would smell like to get the man she wanted. Was it the same for every man? Did they all like the same things?

He didn't read the label and went straight for the sniff. "Yep," he said as he took in the floral and minty notes. "That would work for me."

"Would it?" Olli asked, and Spur dropped the candle in surprise.

The glass shattered on the hard floor, and horror struck Spur right between the ribs. "I'm sorry," he said quickly, taking a step. His cowboy boots crunched over the broken glass though, and he froze again.

He looked from the mess on the floor to Olli, and she burst out laughing. Spur wasn't sure if he should join her or just hold very still while she cleaned up.

"You're digging yourself further and further into the hole," she said as she went into the kitchen. "I mean, I just had the whole house cleaned, and the first thing you do is throw broken glass everywhere." She retrieved a broom and dustpan, giving him a flirty grin while she did.

"I'm sorry," he said again.

She started sweeping up the bigger pieces of glass, and they made tinkling sounds as they touched each other. "You thought it smelled good? That it would've worked for you?"

"Yes," he said carefully, trying not to give too much away.

"What did you like about it?"

"The flowers," he said.

"What else did you smell?" She bent over and swept the pieces into the dustpan, straightened, and paused as she looked at him, waiting for his answer. Her bright eyes were so wide, and she looked like she really wanted to learn from him.

"Something fruity," he said. "Maybe."

"Get Your Man is multi-layered," she said, their eyes never leaving one another. Spur could barely breathe, and the little air he did take in stung his dry throat.

Olli spun away from him and took the glass to the trash can. She got a washcloth from the sink and came back, bending over to wipe the floor all around. Scratching noises met his ears as she picked up small shards of glass with the wet cloth.

She stood again and faced him, her cheeks flaming a little brighter than before. "What else did you get in the candle?"

"That was all," he said. "Maybe something creamy. Milk or something."

"It's whey," she said. "Very subtle, Mister Chappell. I think you get more bonus points for that."

"*More* bonus points?" he asked.

"Yeah, you earned some this morning when you were the one in the garden and not someone from the ranch."

"Good to know," he said, as he'd be back in the morning with the plants he'd ordered at the nursery yesterday.

"Get Your Man has three fruits in it—mango, orange, and grapefruit. They're the ones most associated with crispness and freshness. I call it tutti fruity." She picked up another candle, and this one was Get Your Man too. She pointed to the words he'd bypassed.

Clean, Crisp, and Ripe For a Kiss.

Tutti fruity sat under Crisp.

"The floral scent is part honeysuckle and part rose. It's ripe for a kiss." She smiled at him quickly. "The cleanness comes from that whey you got. It's very subtle, and most people don't know how to identify it. Milk solids are almost sugary. I like the honey whey the best."

Spur liked her the best, and he didn't know how to say it. He didn't know if he even should say it. "These haven't been lit," he said, his voice far too deep as it got stuck behind the emotion in his throat.

She looked up at him, those pretty eyes wide again. "Guess I haven't found a man I want to get."

CHAPTER 7

"You sure?" Spur asked, and Olli dropped her eyes to his mouth to watch him form the words.

"I mean, not that I've invited anyone over for dinner or anything," Olli said, her mind racing. "That's when I'd light one of these." She lifted her eyes back to his, because looking at his lips was far too dangerous. "When I'd ordered in a romantic meal and want to you know. Get him." The last two words came out almost as a squeak, and Olli needed to get in control of herself before she lunged at the cowboy and kissed him.

She set the whole candle back on the entertainment shelf and gave him a wide berth as she went past the full-size couch back to the kitchen. "Thank you for the trivet," she said, picking it up. Her voice came out normal, thank all the stars in the heavens. "I can put the cookies I bake on it."

"Sure," he said. "I kinda feel like you don't need it though,

because you just said you'd order in food for a romantic meal."
He scanned the kitchen behind her. "Do you not cook?"

"Not often," she said. "I do love to bake, though. I make
cookies every Sunday afternoon."

"Do you now?" His dark eyes sparkled like stars in a
midnight sky, and Olli's imagination went wild.

*Diamond Eyes: Mischief, Interest, and Dangerous to Your
Health.*

It would be a purely masculine scent, one that radiated
from Spur's skin and clothes and drove women wild. Instead
of *Diamond Eyes*, she should call it *Get Your Girl*, and men
across the globe would be clamoring to buy the candle and
burn it for the women they wanted.

"Olli?"

She blinked, coming out of the fantasy rabbit hole she'd
fallen into. Spur had somehow moved closer, and Olli hadn't
seen him do it.

"I lost you," he said.

"I was thinking about a candle for men," she said. "*Get
Your Girl.*" She fingered the trivet. "Your eyes reminded me
of..." She didn't know how to finish, because how could she
tell him that when she looked into his eyes, she saw stars? She
couldn't.

Just like she couldn't tell him that when she looked into
his eyes, she saw mischief and interest and danger—and she
wanted all of it and more.

"My eyes?" he asked, his fingertips trailing up the bare skin
on her arm.

Olli shivered at his touch, though it was warm. His hands

were so big, and he likely worked like a dog around that ranch. Yet his skin was soft against hers too.

"We should go to the perfumery," she said. "You promised to help me with the scents, and now I've got a candle in mind." She took a deep breath—big mistake with him so close. Her hormones rattled inside her, and she pushed her hair over her shoulder. "What are you wearing tonight?" She leaned closer, because she could take this embarrassing moment and turn it flirty.

"You smell amazing," she said. "Women like that in a man, by the way. So we need to bottle you all up and get you selling." She waved her fingers up and down in front of his body, smiling for all she was worth.

Spur grinned and chuckled, which was exactly what Olli had been hoping for. "Is that right?"

"That's right, Mister," she said. "You got so many bonus points today already, though, so I'm not sure how many more I can give out." She gave him what she hoped was a sly look out of the corner of her eye as she turned. "Come on. Follow me."

He did, and Olli had barely stepped outside before Spur secured her hand in his. She stumbled, though she was wearing those flat black sandals Ginny had suggested she wear the previous evening.

She looked at their hands, then let her gaze slide up Spur's tanned, muscled forearm to his shoulder, and finally his face.

"I like you, Olli," he said when their eyes met. He wore so much in his expression that Olli couldn't decipher it all.

"Okay?" He lifted her hand to his lips, and fire raced through her skin to her muscles to her veins. "Is this okay?"

"Is what okay?" she whispered, feeling like the weight of gravity had stopped working. She was floating somewhere outside her own reach, and Spur was the only thing tethering her to Earth at all.

"Me holdin' your hand," he said.

"Oh." She looked at where their fingers were intertwined again. "Yeah, it's okay."

"Just okay?" he teased. "Not earning me any bonus points?"

Olli giggled, her brain finally catching up to the situation. "How can I earn bonus points with you?" she asked as she got her feet moving again. Holding hands with Spur—really holding hands with him—made her feel like a million bucks.

I like you, Olli.

She liked him too. How could she make it as obvious for him as he had her? Or had she already?

"You don't need any bonus points, Olli," he said. "I ripped up your flowers. Ruined your product. Broke your candle." He shook his head. "I'm lucky you haven't kicked me back to Bluegrass."

She shook her head, but her smile wouldn't go. "You took me dancing," she said. "Brought me one of your trivets, even after I teased you about the knitting. You've been wearing this super-sexy, clean cowboy hat every time I see you, and you're going to help me with my men's line. I think we're about even."

He reached up and pressed on the "super-sexy" cowboy

hat, and Olli wondered when the last time someone told him he was handsome and desirable. She wanted to tell him.

Her perfumery sat down the lane about three hundred yards, and as they approached, she saw Charity's red Mini Cooper parked out front. A groan gathered in the back of her throat, and Spur either heard it or sensed it.

"What?" he asked.

"Charity comes on Tuesdays to label bottles," she said.

"Who's Charity?"

"She works for me," Olli said. She was normally grateful for the college student who came two or three times a week to help in the perfumery. Olli didn't see her often, and she didn't want to take Spur in to meet the beautiful blonde who peeled and stuck stickers to bottles, printed new labels, fulfilled orders, and anything else that needed to be done during her shift.

She paused on the road in front of the perfumery, and Spur did too. He watched the building for another moment before looking at her. "I like you, too, Spur," she said, employing all of her bravery. Fitting, as she'd spritzed *Take A Chance* in her hair moments before Spur had rung the doorbell.

She felt like she'd just leapt off of a cliff, and she was definitely taking a chance with the handsome cowboy billionaire next door.

"Okay?" she asked.

Spur gave her a tight nod, those midnight eyes lit up from within again. He leaned down, his free hand sliding easily along her waist. Olli's eyes drifted closed; her heartbeat shot through her body at triple its normal speed.

He was going to kiss her. Any moment now, Spur Chappell was going to *kiss her.*

"Olli," Charity called. "I need you in here, stat."

Spur backed up, and Olli opened her eyes. She caught him putting his cowboy hat back on his head as he turned toward the door of the perfumery.

Charity looked like she'd been panicking for a while, and that was when the scent of something burnt and something decayed hit Olli straight in the chest. She gagged and started for the door. A few seconds later, Spur said, "What is that smell?" and Olli wanted to crawl in the nearest hole, call the maid service to come clean up the perfumery, and hide until the mess was cleaned up.

"I don't know what's happening," Charity said. "It was fine when I got here, but then this just started boiling. I didn't even know it was on." She hurried over to one of the testing plates Olli used to heat and mix fragrances.

She'd been using it earlier that day, as she experimented with strawberry and sage. It smelled like manure now. Burnt manure.

"I must have forgotten to turn it off," Olli said, quickly putting on the heat-resistant glove and plucking the vial from the holder over the burner. "It's off now?"

"Yeah," Charity said. "I unplugged it the moment I smelled it. I texted you, but then I saw you out the window."

"Great," Olli said darkly, and she wasn't sure if she was glad Charity had unplugged the burner or seen Spur about to kiss Olli. She put the vial in the sink and turned on the cold water. The glass shattered, and Olli screamed and jumped back.

With the water running and the stench in the air, all of Olli's senses were on full overload. She took a moment to just breathe, and then Spur was there, right at her hip.

"I'll clean up this broken glass," he said, his voice right at her ear. "You go open some windows, okay?"

She looked at him, and he nodded like, *It's okay, Olli. Not a big deal.*

She said, "Thanks, Spur," and went to do what he'd suggested. She had fans in the back too, because sometimes it got really hot in the front of the perfumery. She hauled those out and got them blowing. She used them when she needed to clear the air—literally—so she could work on a new scent.

She sent Charity home and waved to her from the front door. When she turned back to the perfumery, it was just her, Spur, and a lot of open windows.

"I think the smell is mostly gone," he said, looking around as if physical evidence of scent could be found.

"Thanks for helping," she said. "Definitely double bonus points for that."

He smiled, always so sure of himself. Olli envied him for that. "Do you think you can still smell anything?" he asked. "I'm happy to stay and lend my Y-chromosomes."

"We can try," she said. "I really do want to know what cologne you're wearing."

"It's Montana Sky," he said.

She moved closer to him, lifting her chin as she smelled him. "Don't be freaked out by the smelling," she said.

"Too late," he responded, actually inching away from her. She backed him into the sink, finally fisting a handful of his shirt—a deliciously dark blue button-up that had never seen work on a ranch—and holding him in place.

"Smells decidedly blue," she said. "Like the Montana sky. Something peppery in there too." She closed her eyes and cocked her head.

"How does blue have a smell?" he asked.

"Shh," she whispered. "I'm smelling."

"Olli, you smell with your—"

"Shh."

He fell silent, and Olli enjoyed the warmth of his body so close to hers. He really did smell fantastic, and her head swam. Her thoughts swayed even as she tried to grab onto them and hold them still.

"It's cedar," she said, opening her eyes. "Blue smells like linen," she said. "Water. Air. Sky. Clean. Blue is clean."

He looked down at her, and her heartbeat did a stuttering rhythm. "You like this?" he asked.

"Yes," she said, releasing his shirt and backing up. "I was working on something with a spicier scent." She walked away from him, mentally commanding herself to stay in control. Just because he'd held her hand didn't mean they were building a real relationship.

She picked up the vial with the concoction she'd put together last week. "What do you think of this?" She used a cotton swab to put a drop of the liquid on a card. She waved it back and forth to dry and returned to where he stood against the sink, both hands braced at his sides.

"Smell."

He did, his eyes never leaving hers. He didn't like it, she could tell, but she waited for him to say something.

"It's too strong," he said.

"Which part?"

"It smells too much like incense," he said.

"Fair enough." Olli turned around, her hopes sinking. "I have something else." She'd been trying for crisp and clean, musky, and woodsy, yet...artistic. It wouldn't suit someone like Spur, who was more rugged and leathery and cowboy than a man in a business suit. Each man would have his own tastes, and she just needed to find something that would appeal to someone besides her.

She repeated the task of getting the scent card ready and returned to him. "Smell."

He did, and his eyebrows went up. "It's crisp," he said. "Almost alcoholic."

Olli knew he was right, and she nodded, her mouth pressed into a line. "It's too strong too." She turned away from him, wondering why she couldn't find the right notes. "That's all I've got."

"You need something subtle," he said. "Like the honey milk in that candle." He came up beside her, but he didn't touch her. "Start with something warm."

"Cinnamon?" she asked. "Vanilla?"

"Sure," he said. "Make it subtle. Make it carry the other scents, the way you did in the candle."

"What other scents, though?"

"Something crisp," he said. "Clean. Outdoors. Dirty."

"You literally said clean and dirty in the same sentence."

He grinned at her and shrugged. "A man wants to feel like he can take on a wild bear for the woman he loves. That's a dirty job."

"Or maybe you just have a dirty job, so you like the smell of dirt."

He laughed, the sound filling her perfumery. She hoped it would get caught in all the cracks so she could listen to it again later.

"Not dirt," he said. "The *idea* of getting dirty. Like your idea of *A Hopeful Future*."

"So what does that smell like?"

"Pine, and dirt, and sky all at once."

"I don't know how to achieve that."

"Mint, and water, and leather," he said. "Definitely leather."

She looked at him, finding him gorgeous and beautiful for being there with her. He worked long hours, and yet, there he was. Tall and fresh and utterly charming.

"Leather," she said, her mind firing now. "Wood. Maybe... campfire smoke."

"Something smoky," he mused, his eyes turning thoughtful. "That could work, because men like being the king of the grill too."

"I'm not going to make something smell like meat," Olli said, nudging him with her shoulder. "Smoke is an interesting concept though. I wonder if it would pair with an herb." She let her mind wander, and she picked up a pen and started taking notes.

Spur stayed nearby while she did, and when her thoughts finally ran out, she looked up to find him watching her.

"Sorry," she said. "Sometimes I get carried away." She put the pen down. "What time is it?"

"I have no idea," he said, his voice soft.

Olli pulled out her phone and saw it was after nine. Surprised, she looked at Spur. "Why didn't you interrupt me?"

"I liked watching you," he said simply. "You have a unique mind, Olli."

"Is that a compliment?"

"Yes," he said, standing from the stool he'd found. "While you were working, I looked up a couple of things." He turned his phone to face her. "I was thinking we should go to this tomorrow night."

Olli peered at the screen. "A night out in the country." She looked at Spur. "Country music, Spur? Could you be any more cowboy?"

"I sure hope not," he said, grinning. "Glen Ricks is playing, and I love him. He's so good with a guitar. It's only an hour away. I'll take you to dinner, and we'll go to the concert, and you know, there will be a lot of men there. Lots of smelling opportunities." He grinned at her and put his phone in his back pocket.

She considered him, knowing she was going to say yes but wanting to drag out the moment just so he'd know she wasn't really a country music fan. "Country music," she said with a scoff. "It's like you're Texan and not from Kentucky."

He laughed, and Olli joined in with him. "What do you like?" he asked.

"Kentucky bluegrass, of course," she said.

"Perfect," he said. "We'll go to the Monroe Memorial concert next month."

"You're kidding," she said as he stepped into her personal space and wrapped his arms around her. "You can't get tickets to that, Spur. They've been sold out forever."

"Maybe I already have tickets," he said. "You're obviously not the only one who likes bluegrass music in Kentucky."

Olli simply gazed up at him, wondering what was happening right now. Were they a real couple? Had he been about to kiss her earlier? When he said he liked her, did he mean he was interested in her romantically?

How had this relationship bloomed so quickly?

"You don't have to use them on me," she said, coming back to Earth. She stepped delicately out of his arms. "The investor is coming in two weeks. We won't need to pretend to be together next month." She turned her back on him, because until whatever was happening between them was defined, she had to treat him as a fake boyfriend.

"Come on, Olli," he said, a hint of frustration in his voice.

"What?" She didn't turn to look at him.

"Don't do that," he said. "We're too old for games."

Olli picked up the pen she'd been using earlier. Her notes looked more like chicken scratch than human writing, but she could read what she'd scrawled down.

"Olli," he said, taking the pen from her. He used a couple

of fingers to gently lift her chin until she was looking at him. "I said I liked you. That's not pretend."

Olli didn't know what to say.

"You said you liked me," he said. "What did you mean by that?"

She swallowed as he dropped his hand, but she kept her face turned up to his. "What did you mean?"

"I meant that I liked you," he said. "I meant that I don't want this to be pretend."

"What's this?" she asked.

"You and me," he said boldly, actually squaring his shoulders and clenching his jaw. "You and me, Olli. I want *you and me* to be a real couple."

"Not fake," she said, trying to put what he'd said into her own words. "Not pretend, for an investor?"

"No," he said. "I want to hold your hand, and bring you flowers, and take you to dinner. I want to go dancing, and listen to you laugh, and learn everything about you." He took a deep breath. "I want to kiss you, and I want to find out if I can fall in love again."

Olli sucked in a breath, and her eyes widened at his last few words. "Spur."

"Sorry, I said too much," he said, stepping back. "Don't freak out. I just...I *like* you, Olli."

It had been a while since someone had liked Olli. She studied him for a moment, and then swept into his personal space and hugged him tightly. He sighed and relaxed as he wrapped his arms around her too.

"I like you too, Spur," she whispered, equal parts fear and

excitement racing through her veins. She wasn't sure she could perpetuate a real relationship for long. What if Spur learned something about her he didn't like?

Please just let us last until the investor is gone, she thought as she stood in his embrace. After that, if she had to, she could deal with the broken pieces of her heart.

CHAPTER 8

S pur set down the tray of cupcakes when he reached the picnic table. His mother had left a spot for them, and he was actually surprised that she hadn't taped off a section and labeled it desserts.

He loved his mother, but she was a special kind of woman. One who liked every T to be crossed, and every I dotted. Not only that, but she had a specific set of criteria for those cross-ings and dottings, and Spur had always felt like he'd never measure up to her standards. She'd been *most* disappointed when his marriage had fallen apart, but not because it had caused Spur to question everything about himself. Only because of what she had to say to the other ladies at church to make sure the Chappell family name stayed untarnished.

Spur concerned himself with image too, but he honestly did not think anyone outside of Dreamsville or the horse racing world knew his last name. He *knew* they didn't.

"Did you get the buns, baby?" his mother asked, arriving

at the picnic area on the ranch. She'd had it built specifically for family events like this, and Spur couldn't say he hated it. Sometimes he ate lunch here if he wasn't feeling particularly social or if one of his brothers was annoying him.

Right now, everything put him on-edge, and he looked at his mother blankly. "Buns?"

"They were right next to the chips," she said.

"Cayden grabbed the chips," Spur said, looking over his shoulder. He really didn't want to go back to the house where his parents lived. It was all the way on the other side of the ranch, and Olli was supposed to meet him in a few minutes. He looked toward her property, hoping to catch a glimpse of her walking toward him right now.

"Listen, Mom," he said, clearing his throat.

"Duke, call your father and find out if the buns are still on the counter." She turned back to Spur, who thought he might have gone deaf for a moment while she shouted in her high-pitched voice. "What, baby?"

He watched Cayden and Blaine pull to a stop and get out of the truck. They went to the tailgate and picked up a huge cooler, each of them carrying one end. Spur took a deep breath.

"I invited someone to the picnic," he said, looking at his mother.

"Right here, boys," she yelled to Cayden and Blaine. "Trey, go tell Conrad to get off the phone. We're about to start."

They were at least twenty minutes from starting, especially if Daddy was still back at the house for Duke to call. Spur's frustration grew, and he glared at Cayden and Blaine as they set the cooler down where their mother indicated they should.

Blaine was right; Spur should've talked to his mother earlier.

"Conrad's talking to Hilde," Trey called. "He said he'll get off when we actually start."

"That boy," Mom said, shaking her head.

"Hey, he has a girlfriend, Ma," Cayden said. "Isn't that what you're always badgering me to get? A girl?" He slung his arm around his mother's shoulders, but she just gave him a dirty look.

"You had a perfectly good woman, Cayden, and you blew it."

"I did not," Cayden said with a laugh. "I think you need to get your memory checked, Ma. She broke up with me."

"Because you refused to sell a horse," Mom shot back.

Cayden looked at Spur and shook his head. Spur smiled, but he wasn't close to laughing. Mom just didn't get some things. What she did take from a situation was never what Spur saw or felt, and he'd confirmed over and over that men and women were simply different.

"Okay, Ma," Cayden said, moving down to the cupcakes.

"Did you get the buns next to the chips?" Spur asked.

"Yeah," Cayden said. "Blaine tossed them in the back seat."

"Dad says there aren't any buns on the counter," Duke said, reaching for a cupcake.

"Get your hands off." Mom practically shot in front of him, blocking his attempt to reach the sweets.

Spur looked toward Olli's house, wondering why in the world he'd thought this was a good idea. They'd had a great week together. Fantastic, even. Laughing and dancing at the concert. Thursday, he'd actually left the ranch during the day and taken her to lunch. They'd spent that evening in her perfumery again, where she had him smell no less than six new samples.

She was getting closer, that was for sure. He'd never seen anyone think the way she did, and he found her smart, witty, and sexy all in one package.

He had not kissed her yet, because the timing had never felt right. He could still see her with her head tipped back slightly, her eyes closed, standing out in front of her perfumery from Tuesday night. He'd almost kissed her then, but his hesitation had allowed her employee to interrupt them.

He'd been thinking about that hesitation for days now, and he still couldn't name a reason for it.

"Oh, I don't believe this," Mom said, and Spur tore his gaze from the waving grasses between the pavilion and Olli's land. His mother marched down the sidewalk that led to the small parking area. "You were supposed to bring Daddy with you," she said to Ian and Lawrence, the last two brothers to arrive.

"He said he could drive himself," Ian said, ducking sideways to avoid their mother.

"What do you want us to do, Mom?" Lawrence asked, using the slow cooker he carried like a shield. "Throw him kicking and screaming over our shoulders?"

"Yes," Mom said. "He can't drive. The doctor said he has to wait at least another two weeks."

Lawrence put the appliance full of meat next to the empty spot where the buns would clearly go. Neither Blaine nor Cayden had made an attempt to get them, and the brothers that were nearby looked around at each other.

"Mom," Spur said, because it always fell to him to have delicate conversations with their mother. "We can't control Daddy."

"Oh, I know," she said, waving one perfectly manicured hand. "That man is as stubborn as the day is long." She pointed around at everyone, even Conrad though he stood several paces away with his back to her. "You all are exactly the same way."

"Hey," Ian said. "I'm not."

No one else argued, and Spur just shook his head. "Listen, Mom, did you hear what I said a few minutes ago?"

"No, what?" She couldn't hold still for more than three seconds, and Spur sighed as she started straightening already perpendicular serving utensils.

He exchanged a glance with Blaine and then Trey. "I invited someone to the picnic," Spur said, his voice too loud when the breeze suddenly died. "A woman, Mom. I invited a woman to the picnic."

His mother froze, and though Spur could only see her profile, he felt the shock rolling off of her in waves. She straightened slowly and faced him. "Who?" she asked.

"Yeah," Ian said. "Who?"

"You're dating?" Lawrence asked, and Spur shot them both a look that said, *not helping. Be quiet.*

"Duke and Conrad brought dates," Spur said. "I didn't think it was a big deal."

His mother's eyebrows went up. "You didn't think inviting an outsider to our *family* picnic was a big deal? What if I'd made the exact number of cupcakes?"

"She can have mine," Spur said, growing more agitated by the moment. "Look, it's not a big deal, okay? It's new, and I thought she should meet everyone at once so she can decide if she wants to keep dating me."

"You're supposed to hide all the flaws until after the wedding," Trey joked.

"Hey," Mom said. "We are not flaws. We are your family."

"They're both F-words," Trey said, laughing.

Mom was not laughing, and she looked back at Spur. "Who is she, darling? Do we know her?"

"Yeah," Spur said, glancing to the right again. This time, he saw Olli headed his way. Relief and fear ran through him together. "Uh, she's right there, Mom. It's Olivia Hudson." He pointed to the right, and everyone turned that way.

Seven sets of eyes landed on Olli, and she actually slowed her step. Spur realized what a horrible thing he'd done, but it was too late now.

"Olli?" Lawrence and Ian said together, equal amounts of disbelief in their voices.

"She's great," Blaine said, and Spur was never more thankful for him.

"Yeah," Trey said. "I like Olli a lot. She's real pretty, too, Spur. How'd you get her to go out with you?"

"Duke's stupid sheep tore up her flowers," Spur said, and at least that was true.

"I said I was sorry about that," Duke said, still staring in Olli's direction. "But hey, if it brought you two together, I should get credit."

Spur was well-aware that his mother had still said nothing, her eagle eyes trained on Olli as she picked her way through the last of the wild grass. He moved toward her then, an apology on the tip of his tongue.

"Hey," he said, glad when his voice came out smooth and easy. He embraced her and whispered, "I just want to say I'm sorry in advance."

She pulled back slightly and looked at him. "You're sorry?"

"I maybe didn't tell anyone that you were coming until sixty seconds ago."

"No wonder they're looking at me like I'm fresh meat and they're hungry lions." She stepped all the way back and gave herself a little shake. "It's fine. We can do this."

He wanted to ask her, *Do what?*, but she put her hand in his and stepped forward, leaving him no choice but to go with her.

He remembered his Southern manners, and said, "Olli, this is my mother, Julie Chappell."

"So nice to see you again, ma'am," Olli said, a bright, white smile on her face.

His mother blinked, but she shook Olli's hand.

Spur kicked himself into gear again. "I know you've met

all the brothers at some point, but there are a lot of them. Let's just go around." He looked at Blaine, who stood closest to their mother. "Blaine. He's one of the middle brothers."

"Heya, Olli."

"Ian's the other one of those." Spur turned around to point out Ian. Honestly, if he were Olli, he'd be confused already. They all wore blue jeans and cowboy hats. Heck, Ian and Duke were both wearing a red shirt.

"Then we've got the younger brothers. Duke is the wee youngest. His girlfriend will be here soon."

Duke grinned and lifted his hand as if Spur was doing roll call. "Let's see...Conrad is next. He's talking to his girlfriend. Then there's Lawrence." He turned her back to Blaine. "And the older brothers are Trey and Cayden—he's the same age as you—and me."

"Nice to meet you all," Olli said. "I mean, we've met, obviously, but yes. Nice to see you all again."

Everyone seemed made of happy-happy smiles, and Spur didn't know what to say next. His father's truck came into view, and Mom sprang into action. "Conrad," she said, marching toward him. "If you don't hang up in the next five seconds, I will throw that phone in the duck pond."

"All right, Mom," he said. "Calm down."

"I will not calm down." She looked over her shoulder. "Spur, you and Cayden get down to the lot and help your father. If he gets re-injured, so help me..." She didn't finish the threat, and Spur wondered why she couldn't act normal for just one meal.

He met Olli's gaze and asked, "See why I apologized in advance?"

She just blinked, looking like someone had hit her with a baseball bat.

Spur sighed. "Come on, Cayden. Let's go make sure Daddy doesn't get us in trouble." He kept hold of Olli's hand and towed her with him. He wasn't going to leave her to the wolves dressed in his brothers' clothing, that was for dang sure.

Katie had told him once that his family was a lot to handle, especially all at the same time. Spur had believed her, but he didn't really understand until they got divorced. He'd always been around this massive group of people with loud voices and strong opinions, so he didn't know what it was like to not fit in.

"Hey, Daddy," he said as his dad opened the door. "Real quick, this is Olivia Hudson."

"Oh, hello," Daddy said, his smile genuine.

Spur reached for his arm, and Cayden darted into the open doorway too. Olli got jostled back as they tried to help their father out of the truck in such a way that he wouldn't get re-injured. He'd had hip surgery only two weeks ago, and his recovery had been slow and somewhat painful.

They finally got him to the ground, Spur noticing just how heavily his dad was leaning on him. His grip on Spur's bicep was strong, and Spur made sure he didn't let go. He found his feet and looked at Olli again. "It's nice of you to join us. Did you make a cake or something?"

Horror washed through Spur. "No, Daddy, she's here,

because she's my girlfriend." He cut a glance at her and looked quickly back to his father.

"She is not," Daddy said with a laugh.

"I didn't think so either, Jefferson," Mom said, and Spur looked at her too. She wore displeasure on her face, and Spur really wished she'd learned how to lighten up in the seventy years she'd been on this planet. "But that's what the boy says." She linked her arm through Daddy's, and Spur fell back.

"I'm not a boy," he called after them, but neither one of them turned around or acknowledged him. He felt like a misbehaving fourteen-year-old, despite Cayden's clap on his shoulder. Dejected, Spur stood there, wondering what they'd expected to see between him and Olli that they hadn't demonstrated.

Olli slipped her fingers between Spur's, and the two of them stood there, watching as everyone came together for the picnic. Duke looked around, and he trotted down to the lot with a grin when Allison arrived. He pulled her from her car with a growl, and she squealed as he kissed her.

"He's thirteen years younger than me," Spur said, watching them. "We don't have to act like that."

"I would shoot you dead if you growled at me," Olli said.

Their eyes met, and Spur had time to inhale before she started laughing. He joined her, easily putting his arm around her waist as she leaned into him.

Something nagged at him still, because he and Olli needed to convince a stranger that they were falling for one another in just one week. If he couldn't even convince his parents, what chance did he have of fooling a businessman?

You're not trying to fool anyone, he told himself as his mom gestured wildly for Duke and Allison, and Spur and Olli to join them under the pavilion. *This is real, Spur. You both agreed it was real.*

If it was, why did everything still feel fake? Why did he feel like he needed to prove to his mom and dad that he was dating Olli?

He didn't know, but he thought about it through the prayer, and while he put food on his plate. He looked at Olli as he sat across from her, and his blood turned to liquid lava. He *liked* her. He just had to figure out how to make sure everyone around them knew it, so she could get the grant she wanted.

If she lost that because his performance wasn't convincing enough, Spur knew it wouldn't matter how much he liked her. She'd kick him to the curb and send him a bill for taking up the last two weeks of her precious time.

"Where did you guys go on your first date?" Ian asked as he sat next to Olli.

She looked at him, half-smiling though her mouth was full of food. "Six Stars."

"Is that right?" Ian asked, looking at Spur. He could tell what was going to come out of his brother's mouth before he even opened it.

"Don't," Spur growled.

Ian grinned for all he was worth.

"What's...what?" Olli looked between Spur and Ian, still smiling herself.

"Just that Spur takes all of his first dates to Six Stars," Ian said, popping a potato chip in his mouth. "He likes to impress the ladies with his dancing."

"That's not true," Spur said as Olli looked at him, her eyebrows up, though it pretty much was. Could he help it if women liked a man who could dance? No, he could not.

"Name the last woman you went out with where your first date *wasn't* at Six Stars," Ian challenged.

"Name the last woman you went out with," Spur shot back, darkness gathering in his soul.

"Theresa," Ian said without missing a beat. He grinned and turned fully to Olli. "What else has dear Spur done for your dates?"

"Enough," Spur said, shooting a glance a couple of places down where their mother sat. He leaned forward and glared at Ian, his voice soft as he asked, "Why aren't you on my side here?"

Ian laughed, and Cayden bumped into him from behind, sending him toward the table. "Hey," he said.

"Oops," Cayden said, looking at Spur and not Ian. "Sorry." He clearly wasn't sorry, and he'd obviously bumped Ian on purpose.

Spur wanted to thump him over the head, and the only thing he could think about was how dysfunctional his family could be sometimes.

"Ian," Olli said. "You're one of the brothers that was married. Like Spur." She looked at him with innocent eyes, but Spur knew her a little better than that. "Right?"

The laughter fell from Ian's countenance. His wife of only six months had only married him for his money, and she'd left huge gashes on his heart. He still wasn't over Minnie, and Spur knew exactly how that felt.

He'd tried to talk to Ian about it, but his younger brother didn't want Spur's advice or commiseration. They'd actually drifted further apart instead of bonding the way Spur would've liked.

He watched his brother struggle to even breathe, and Spur knew the awful way that pinched in a man's chest. "Olli," he said quietly. "It wasn't..." He shook his head.

"Oh, I'm sorry," Olli said, and she sounded like she meant it too. She patted Ian's arm, and he just nodded. "Really, Ian. I didn't know."

"It's okay," Ian said, looking from her to Spur. Something brotherly did pass between them then, and Spur thought maybe this picnic wouldn't go completely up in flames.

Then his mother turned to Cayden, who'd sat on the other side of Olli, and asked, "Why didn't you ever think to ask out Olivia Hudson? She's just been next door for ages."

"Oh, Mom," Cayden said with a laugh. "No one goes looking for their soulmate right next door."

Spur sucked in a breath as Olli lowered her head.

Cayden froze, his eyes growing wide. "I mean..."

Tension rode the air currents, and Spur couldn't get himself to take another bite of food. "Cayden, just let it be," he said quietly. If they'd all stop engaging with their mother, maybe she'd stop eventually too.

"I'm sorry," Olli said, looking at Cayden. She held up her phone. "I just got an emergency text from my floor manager. I can't stay." She started to rise, and Spur's desperation knocked against all of his ribs.

He half-rose too. "Olli," he said.

"It's fine, Spur," she said, but she wouldn't meet his eyes. She also sounded one breath away from crying, and he really couldn't let her walk away in that state. "You stay. Really. Sometimes these things happen when you're running a two million dollar business by yourself." She glared down the table to his mother, who didn't even look up from her plate.

Spur lifted one leg over the bench to go with her. He even said, "Let me walk you back."

"No," Olli practically barked at him. "It's fine. Really. I'm fine." With that, she walked away, her back straight and her head held high.

Spur could only stare at her back, wishing he'd had a chance to tell her how amazing she looked in those white shorts and that dark blue tank top. She wore a pair of tennis shoes and her hair in a curly ponytail that had smelled like summer sunshine and warm fruit. She'd probably named it *Family Picnics and Happy Couples* or something equally as amazing as she was.

"Sit down, baby," his mother said. "She'll be okay."

Spur looked at his mother, still in a bit of a trance. "I'm not hungry," he said. "Excuse me."

"It's a *family* picnic," his mom said as he freed himself from the confining picnic table. "Spur."

"If he's leaving, can I go?" someone asked, and Spur's guilt punched him in the back of the throat.

He turned back to everyone, wondering when he'd

WINNING THE COWBOY BILLIONAIRE   99

stopped being respected. "Duke and Conrad have their girl-friends here," he said calmly. "What's the big deal if I invite mine?"

"No big deal," Cayden said. "Right, everyone?"

"Not to me," Trey said. "I think she's really sweet."

"I didn't mean to upset her," Ian said. "I was just kidding."

"He has a point," Duke said, his eyes worried.

"Darling," his mother said. "Just get a cupcake and come sit down. You'll call her later, and it'll be okay."

Spur wanted to lift up the tray of cupcakes he'd carried to the table and throw it as far as he could. Instead, he did what his mother said, because he didn't want to cause a scene. At least more of a scene than had already been caused.

He kept his head down and his mouth shut for the rest of the picnic, and as he helped clean up, he stuck close to Cayden, Blaine, and Trey. He wanted to ask them if it was that obvious that he and Olli weren't a very strong couple, but he didn't. He didn't need the extra salt rubbed into already open wounds.

CHAPTER 9

Olli expected Spur to show up on Sunday. She'd refused to take his calls on Saturday evening, and instead, she'd texted to say she didn't feel well and was going to bed early. He'd texted and asked if she'd feel better for church in the morning, and she'd said no.

She'd actually told the man no.

The fact that he'd invited her to church spoke volumes. Around these parts, if a man took a woman to church with him, it was almost as good as a proposal. Spur surely knew the culture of Dreamsville, as he'd lived here for his whole life, just like her.

He'd stopped texting after that, saying he wouldn't bother her so she could go to bed and start feeling better.

Olli had laid in bed for a long time last night. She'd eaten almost an entire bag of potato chips, and then three of the frozen peanut butter cookies from her freezer. She kept them for real emergencies, and such a spectacular failure in front of Spur's whole family felt like a state of emergency to her.

She woke sweating and with a sugar hangover, but she didn't care. She'd shower to shake off the night sweats that came from eating too much so close to bedtime, and she was already planning to make more cookies that afternoon. Her Sunday ritual wouldn't be swayed by a handsome cowboy, clean boots, and a sexy hat.

Her doorbell rang just after noon, and Olli looked toward the heavy front door. She hadn't started the cookies yet, but she suddenly wanted a whole dozen to herself. She hadn't showered yet, and she hadn't even gotten dressed.

"He's already seen you in such a state," she said, but she didn't move from where she'd been lying on the couch. Something played on the TV in front of her, but she didn't know what.

Yesterday afternoon, after she'd stomped home from the humiliating picnic, she'd lit every candle in her house and let them burn for hours and hours. They'd filled the space with far too much perfume, and Olli had opened all the windows last night to get the smell out.

"I know you're in there," Ginny called. "I have a device locator on your phone, and it says you're here."

Olli sighed as she got off the couch. She padded over to the door, her bathrobe swinging around her legs as she walked. She opened the door a few inches and stuck her head in the gap. "You have a device locator on my phone?"

"Of course," Ginny said, like not having one would be ridiculous. "I'm your emergency person, Olli. What if something happens to you, and no one can find you?" She held up her fancy phone. "I'd be able to, and I'd be touted as the hero who helped the police find your body." She grinned. "Now, come on. Let me in. It's hot out here."

Olli sighed a big sigh, but she stepped back and let the door settle open.

"Why are you not even dressed?" Ginny asked. "You didn't go to church today?"

"No," Olli said. "I'm the devil. Sue me."

Ginny watched her with narrowed eyes, then turned back to close the door. She set her purse on the table by the door and gasped. "You burned *Get Your Man*." She peered over Olli's shoulder to the hall that led back into the bedrooms. With wide eyes and a hushed voice, she asked, "Is Spur here?"

"No," Olli said, returning to the couch. She flopped back onto the pillows she'd put there, wondering why Spur hadn't come yet. Church had surely ended an hour ago. Maybe he had more family obligations today.

Those Chappells...Olli wasn't sure what to think.

Ginny perched on the edge of the recliner and looked at Olli. Her gaze was almost as heavy as all seven of Spur's brothers, and his mother. "What happened?"

"I don't want to talk about it," Olli said, staring at the cheetah on the screen. She didn't even know what channel she was on. She'd considered texting Spur that they were done. The charade was over, and he could stop telling her he liked her. She'd find someone else to help her fool Mr. Renlund, and she'd get the grant.

Easy.

"Okay, this is not okay." Ginny got up and turned off the TV. "You're watching Animal Planet, Olli. *Animal Planet.*"

"So what?"

"You skipped church. You're not dressed. Every single one of these candles has been burned." She picked up one jar and then another. "You don't have butter softening on the counter for oatmeal cookies, and you don't want to talk about it? You get ready to talk about it, or I'm calling...someone, and we're going to take you to the hospital for professional psychiatric help."

Olli smiled at her. "That almost sounded like a real threat."

"It is a real threat," Ginny said, her voice a bit haughty.

"You'd have really pulled it off if you knew who to call to take me to the psychiatric unit at the hospital." Olli giggled, and that got Ginny to crack a smile.

"I could call Elliott," Ginny said, and that was a real threat.

"You wouldn't dare," Olli said.

"Not if you get up and get dressed and tell me what's going on."

"Fine." Olli got herself into a seated position. "This requires hot water and eucalyptus." She started down the hall to the master bedroom, Ginny in her wake.

She got in the shower, and Ginny sat on the closed toilet in the separate room. While Olli stood in the hot spray, the misty eucalyptus coming up to greet her, her mind cleared. She started the story with, "He didn't even tell his family about us until one minute before I got there."

That had caused a slight sting in Olli's chest, if she were

being honest with herself. He'd told her about the picnic five days ago. He'd known she was coming, and he'd belonged to his family for forty-six years. He hadn't anticipated their reaction to him bringing a woman to their family picnic?

Was he embarrassed of her? Had he been lying every day this week when he said he liked her, when he called her beautiful, or when he held her hand?

If he had, he was a very, very good liar.

"I don't think Spur would do that," Ginny said, and Olli realized she'd vocalized every question and all of her insecurities. She hadn't even started washing her hair yet, either, so she focused on that while Ginny spit out reassurance after reassurance.

Olli got out of the shower and wrapped a towel around herself. Ginny came out and stood just behind her. Their eyes met in the mirror. "You really like this man," Ginny said softly.

Olli could only nod.

"Come on," Ginny said, gently turning her. "You go put on something that makes you feel sexy and powerful. I'll braid your hair, and we'll make cookies. Then, we'll take them to Spur and see how he reacts to a gorgeous, brilliant woman who shows up with chocolate."

Ginny's dark eyes sparkled, and Olli was so grateful for her. She hugged her best friend tightly, and said, "Thank you, Ginny."

"Don't thank me yet," she said. "I'm going to make you deviate from your recipe schedule." She nodded as she started to leave the bathroom. "I'll go make sure you have the ingredients for fudgeys."

"It's oatmeal this week," Olli said, but she knew she wouldn't win against Ginny. She did love fudgeys, and they were twice as chocolatey as any other recipe Olli had.

She got dressed in the sexy white shorts she'd worn to the picnic yesterday—Spur hadn't even commented on them—and skipped the navy tank top she'd chosen just for him. Instead, she put on a red t-shirt with a whitewashed heart across the chest and went out into the kitchen.

Ginny looked up from the recipe book and surveyed Olli's fashion choice. "Those shorts are amazing."

"Thanks," Olli said, finally feeling an inkling of a smile returning to her face.

"Sit." Ginny rounded the island and pulled out a barstool. "Two braids or one?"

"Two," Olli said. She loved wearing braided pigtails, and she didn't care if she was a little too old to pull off the look. She wasn't going to the mall to hang out. She was going to make cookies and maybe walk down to her perfumery, and then go back to bed.

Ginny's slender fingers were cool and quick, and she braided Olli's hair while she talked about a man she'd met at the homeowner's association meeting she'd attended last night. Olli had gotten several texts close to midnight about Curtis, so this wasn't news to her, but she did ask a few questions.

"You're dancing around it," Olli said as Ginny put the rubber band on the end of the second braid. "Are you going out with him or what?"

"Yes," Ginny said with a smile. She wouldn't look at Olli as she set the comb on the counter next to the brush. She cut a glance at her out of the corner of her eye. "Tonight, in fact. I also may have told him I had an amazing friend who made the best chocolate fudge cookies in the entire South."

Olli burst out laughing, and that further cleansed her soul. She stood up and hugged Ginny again, both of them giggling. "Fine. You win. Do I have everything for fudgeys?"

"Yes, you do," Ginny said. "I took the liberty of getting most of it out."

"How kind of you," Olli said dryly. She went into the kitchen and tied an apron around her waist while Ginny took the barstool she'd just been sitting on.

An hour later, she had thirty fudgeys and a new outlook on the week. She could find someone to be her fake boyfriend by Friday. Heck, she could put it out on the Internet tonight and have men calling in the morning. Some people would do anything for a job.

"Good luck," she said as Ginny took her foil-wrapped plate of fudgeys. "Have fun. Call me tonight, when you get home." They embraced again, and Ginny left. Olli stood with her hand on the doorknob until her friend got behind the wheel and backed out of the long driveway.

Then she closed the door, retraced her steps to the remaining fudgeys, and stacked three on top of one another for herself. She stood in the kitchen and ate them, trying to decide if she should go to the perfumery or just get back on the couch.

Her doorbell rang, and she turned toward it, expecting Ginny to hurry in and say she'd forgotten something. She didn't, and the doorbell pealed again. This time, someone with very big hands also knocked on the door.

Olli's pulse started to bounce around inside her chest, because she only knew one person with big hands who could be knocking on her door right now.

She strode over to it and opened it to find Spur standing there. He balanced a plate of cookies in one hand while his other was about to knock again.

"Oh, hey." He lowered his hand, pure anxiety in those delicious eyes. "I remembered you said you made cookies on Sunday afternoon, and I was hoping I'd have beaten you to it." He lifted his eyes over her head, his nose working. "But I can smell the fact that I'm too late. Again."

Olli couldn't believe he was standing there. He'd let her walk away yesterday afternoon, and he hadn't insisted on coming over last night. He'd let her use her excuses and put distance between them. She looked at the plate of cookies, and they looked more like sad hockey pucks with a few bits of chocolate clinging to them.

"I hate to break it to you," she said slowly. "But those are not cookies."

Their eyes met, and he started chuckling. Olli couldn't hold her laughter in either, and suddenly it didn't matter that his father hadn't believed for a moment that they were dating. It didn't matter if he took all of his first dates to Six Stars. It didn't matter that she'd embarrassed herself and Ian, even though he'd started it.

She stepped back, and Spur came inside. While she closed the door, he put the hockey pucks on the counter. She turned around, and he was there, ready and willing to take her into his arms.

She stepped into them, because she wanted to. She drew in a long, deep breath of him, and she really, really wanted to craft a candle that smelled like this amazing man.

Strength, she thought. *Security. Sexy Cowboy.*

It would have a subtle peppery note for strength, with the crisp, clean "blue" scent she loved about him as security.

Cotton, she thought, finally naming the crisp note she loved so much. *And sky. Clouds. Cotton clouds.* The final scent for Sexy Cowboy would be leather and horse. Something musky and masculine without being acidic.

It would be an instant bestseller, and women all over the world would be burning it to be reminded of the man of their dreams.

She'd name it Spur.

"I'm sorry about the picnic," he said. "I wasn't sure if I should chase after you or sit down."

"It's okay," Olli said, exhausted. "I don't need to talk about it."

"I do," Spur said. "Is that okay? Can I just talk out loud for a minute?"

Olli slid her fingers along the back of his neck, feeling his hair there. "Sure," she said. "Then you can tell me about your haircut."

A smile graced his handsome face. "I did that for my mother and the picnic."

"Mm."

"Anyway," Spur said, clearing his throat. His hands were

heavy on her waist, and Olli sure did like them. "I'm sorry. My family can be a bit much sometimes, and I've had words with all of them."

Olli let her eyes drift closed as she rested her cheek against his chest. "My parents claim to just be surprised that I'm dating again," he said. "It didn't have anything specifically to do with you."

"Okay." She ran her fingertip along the curve of his ear and listened to his heartbeat pick up the pace. She liked that too.

"Ian felt stupid for calling me out about Six Stars, but he's right. I do take every woman there on a first date. It's *easy* for me," he said. "In a world where dating is not easy for me."

"I don't care about Six Stars," Olli said. "I hope we can go again. I love the food there, and you can dance, cowboy." She leaned back and smiled up at him.

He grinned down at her too. "I don't care what my mother thinks," he said. "All that matters to me is that *we're* honest with each other." He kneaded her closer to him again. "Me and you. Us."

"I can agree to that," she said, letting him wrap his strong arms around her and sway with her while she breathed in the scent of him.

"This is me being honest," he said. "This is real for me. When I introduced you as my girlfriend, that's what you are."

Olli's pulse crashed against her ribs. "Me too, Spur. This is real for me too."

"Good," he said. "Then nothing else matters."

"Oh, something else matters," Olli said, stepping away

from him though she'd like to stay right next to him for a lot longer. "What do you think of these shorts?"

She watched his eyes slip down to her legs, and she saw the slow swallow as it moved through his throat. "They're amazing," he said, finally returning his gaze to hers.

Olli grinned at him as her hip cocked. "One more thing: These cookies. What did you *do* to these?"

CHAPTER 10

Spur walked into the barn the following day and opened the fridge they kept in the office there. All of the brothers used the office, but Lawrence, Trey, and Cayden definitely did the most. When Spur opened the fridge, he found brown bags with names on them inside, and he sifted through them until he found his.

It was always in the back, because no one made it out to the ranch before Spur. He settled on the edge of the desk and opened his bag. A big, round, fudgey cookie sat there, and Spur's smile burst across his face.

He was totally eating dessert first today.

He'd just polished off the delicious cookie, his thoughts racing around Olli and how he could see her that night, when Blaine walked into the office. "Heya," he said, but he didn't look or sound happy.

"What's wrong with you?" Spur asked.

"Nothing." Blaine kept his back turned to Spur as he got

out his lunch. "Listen, All For Glory got another clean bill of health. I took the vet off her, because she seems fine now."

"Okay," Spur said. "If you're sure."

"I'm sure," Blaine said, his brown bag crinkling as he dug into it. "I'm late for a meeting about that hoof rot. I'll catch up to you later for a report."

"Yep," Spur said. "I want to hear about that."

Blaine left the office as quickly as he'd entered, and Spur thought there was definitely something going on. Blaine wasn't one to say until he was ready, though, and Spur respected his brother enough to give him the space he required.

He worked with their veterinarians, vet techs, and medical staff at the ranch. He oversaw the care of all the animals, and he knew more about diseases and infections than any person should have to.

Spur put such things out of his mind so he could finish his lunch, still no closer to a reason to call Olli and ask to see her.

"Just call and ask to see her," he muttered to himself. "You're dating. You don't need a sneaky reason."

Her four o'clocks had come in last week, and he'd spent a morning putting them in the ground for her. She'd brought him coffee and toast, and they'd talked while she sat by him as he worked. He'd liked the simple get-together, and hoped she'd do the same when her gardenias finally came in.

He was just about to call her when his phone chimed. Her name sat on the screen, and he swiped to get to the message. *Just found out that Mr. Renlund will be here on Saturday! He wants to see the perfumery at two, talk to me, and take us to dinner. Does that work for you?*

Yes, Spur typed as quickly as he could. He could practically feel Olli's nerves from here, and he instinctively looked west, toward her house and land. He couldn't see through walls, though, so he refocused on his phone. *I'll be there. It's going to be great.*

Thank you, Spur.

Feeling brave, and while he obviously had her on the phone, he hit the call button. Her line rang, and he paced in the small office.

"Mister Chappell," she said, laughing afterward. "What can I do for you?"

Her laugh made him relax and smile. "I wondered what you were doing tonight," he said.

"Tonight." She exhaled heavily. "Nothing."

"Are you at the perfumery right now?"

"Yes, sir."

"I was thinking we should go to a movie," he said. "Or just dinner. Or dinner *and* a movie. I'd love to take you to Bluegrass Music Hall of Fame and Museum in Rosine, but that's pretty far for a weeknight."

He stopped talking, because he didn't want to babble.

"I get one of those food baskets delivered every other Monday," Olli said, her voice thoughtful. "How about I cook us dinner with that, and you take us to the movie?"

"I can agree to that," he said, grinning. Dinner at Olli's house. Even better than going out, in Spur's opinion.

"Okay," Olli said cheerfully. "Why don't you give me a

few more hours today and I'll see where I'm at? Then I'll know what time I'll be able to close up here and get dinner started."

"Sure thing," he said. "See you later, Olli."

She said goodbye, and Spur ended the call. He'd dated before. He'd been married before. He still felt like he was walking on clouds and marshmallows as he left the office and got back to work on the ranch.

"You're going to kiss her tonight," he told himself as he pushed through the doors and went outside.

"You haven't kissed her yet?" Trey asked, and Spur cursed himself for talking out loud before checking to see if anyone was around. Trey stood just outside the barn, a clipboard in his hand. He studied it, but Spur knew he could wait forever for an answer. Trey had the most patience out of any of the brothers, that was for sure.

He had to, to work with all the people coming and going from the ranch. That was a nightmare for Spur, who much preferred to work alone and check things off with someone than have to have conversations all dang day.

Trey finished his note and looked up as a trainer approached. He handed him the clipboard, and the man signed. "Thanks, Hal," Trey said. "You're good for the rest of the summer, all right? Don't let one of my girls call you and say otherwise."

"Got it, Trey," Hal said, and Trey turned to Spur. "You and Olli haven't...you know."

"It's called kissing," Spur said darkly.

Trey grinned at him. "Hey, I'm actually on your side here.

I think it's great you're dating her. I meant it when I said she was pretty."

"Yeah." Spur sighed. "I know. Sorry, Trey."

"You're worked up over her." Trey gestured down the even, graded path. "Walk with me. I have to get over to the row houses to check on the Whitehouse Ranch."

"Yeah? Why?" Spur easily fell into step with his brother. Everything about him was a little more even than Spur. He laughed easier. He had lighter hair and eyes. He could relax when Spur stayed tense. He let go of emotions while Spur kept them bottled tight. He consciously told himself to breathe out and let the tension go with the air, and it actually worked.

When he remembered to do the things he'd learned in therapy years ago, he felt better.

"There's a rumor Kali Whitehouse has been doubling up her horses," Trey said with a hint of frustration in his voice. "Which means she owes us more money."

"Can't house horses here without paying," Spur said.

"Not only that, but if the Association found out, we could lose our credibility. We need that to keep our prices high, and I'm not willing to risk it for the Whitehouses."

"They've been boarders for decades," Spur said, glancing at Trey. "Are we really going to ask her to leave?"

"No," Trey said. "We're going to ask her how many horses she's got here and see if it corresponds with how many stalls she's paying for." He sounded so calm about it too. "If it doesn't match up, she'll pay for what she's not and move her horses into the appropriate facilities. We can't have it reported that we're cramming animals into too-small spaces, Spur."

"No, I know," Spur said. "I'm with you."

Trey nodded and kept on toward the far row house. Spur had work to do in the exercise arena, so he ducked in there with a, "Good luck, Trey. Let me know how it goes." He worked with the championship horses the Chappells were hoping to sell at the next sales event, and he needed to check with another trainer. When he wasn't doing that, he got reports from everyone else on the ranch, compiled all the information together, and ensured the ranch kept operating at peak efficiency.

Sometimes he didn't know what to do with the information he got. He'd call Daddy then, and his father would walk him through what the best solution was. Spur probably needed to get over to the house where his parents lived now and do a little more explaining when his mother wasn't so stressed and his father wasn't caught off-guard.

He did love his parents, but they'd always been extraordinarily busy, and he'd often felt overlooked. He'd never caused any trouble like Ian and Duke, and Spur had never given his parents any attitude, the way Conrad did.

As a result, his mother hadn't had to spend much time and energy on him growing up. He'd thought he'd been doing her a favor by getting his chores done and keeping up in his classes. He probably had been, but he felt like the cost had been high for him personally.

He pushed his mother out of his mind as he approached the stall where his horse for the afternoon waited for him. "All right Lucky Number Thirteen," he said. "Are you ready for this?"

He grinned at the horse and stepped over to a cooler at the end of the row. He found a bit of carrot and half an apple inside, and he took them to the beautiful black and white horse who could literally win everything next year. "You have to run," he told her. "You have to run when I say, and pull back when I say, and you have to want it more than every other horse out there."

He always gave pep talks to his horses. He believed they could feel his energy and knew on some level what he was telling them.

"You're better than all of them," he said, stroking his hand down the side of her face as she crunched through the apple, core and all. "You act like it, okay? You're going to be the one they're all watching." He smiled as her lips rippled, her signal that she'd like the carrot now, please.

Spur gave it to her and said, "I'm getting the saddle. Get ready."

* * *

By the time Spur showered and put on his dating clothes, the sun was starting to set. Olli had texted for an eight o'clock dinner time, and he'd said they wouldn't be able to make it to a movie if they ate that late.

She'd responded with, *We'll have a movie night in*, and a smiley face.

Spur's heart raced through his chest, much the same way Lucky had galloped around the track together. She'd ran, and Spur was confident he could sell her for a three-quarters of a million dollars. Her mother had won the Preakness three years ago, and her father had qualified for the Derby.

Everyone already knew about Lucky, because it had been a big news event when Here For Good had been brought in to Bluegrass Ranch for the studding. News vans had followed his horse trailer from the ranch where he'd retired, and Spur had turned them away at the gates of Bluegrass.

He got a couple of hours with the horse, and he wanted to make sure his mare got pregnant. No news crews needed for that.

Before he knew it, he stood on Olli's porch once again. If she knew how hard it was to come to the door and ring that blasted bell, she'd have the door open for him before he got there.

"No!" he heard behind the door, and he instinctively leaned closer to it to hear more. "Witcher, you naughty thing. No!"

Spur pressed the button to ring the bell, and Olli appeared only a few seconds later. She sighed as she pushed her hair off her forehead. "Hey, come in."

"Don't sound so happy about it," he teased.

"My stupid cat ate the fish," she said, giving him a disgruntled look as she went past him.

"I can call for delivery," he said easily.

"I promised you dinner," she said, her voice full of helplessness.

"Animals are unpredictable," Spur said.

Olli turned back to him. "You've told me that before. Last week, when the sheep nearly trampled me."

Spur looked up from his phone, where he'd been looking up delivery times for his favorite places. He blinked and then started laughing. "They wouldn't have touched you," he said. "Sheep are scared of their own shadow."

Olli smiled, at least. "Why did you ride in on your big horse then?" She practically prowled toward him, and Spur forgot all about delivery and his phone as he drank in her feminine form. She wore a black pencil skirt that fell tastefully to her knees and gave her an hourglass shape in her hips and waist and bust.

The black and white striped blouse was open at the throat, and Spur tried to imagine what she'd taste like in that spot. His mind blanked when he caught the scent of her perfume, because it was so sexy and so perfect for a woman like Olli.

"Huh?" She tiptoed her fingers up the front of his shirt, and Spur could only look at her. He'd forgotten the question and everything.

He hadn't forgotten what he'd promised himself he'd do that night, and he easily took Olli into his arms, bent his head toward her, and paused.

Her eyes closed, and Spur took that as permission. He still took a moment to remove his hat and ask, "Can I kiss you, Olli?"

"Yes, please," she whispered, and then Spur didn't waste another moment. He let his eyes drift closed too, so he could experience Olli with just taste, sound, touch, and smell.

She tasted like butter and garlic, and Spur sure did like that. He heard himself make a little groan, and he felt Olli's fingers move through his hair. He breathed in through his nose, getting that delicious scent of something floral and something clean and something maybe a little spicy. No matter what, her perfume drove him to deepen the kiss, and he was glad he'd remembered how to kiss a woman without making a complete fool of himself.

CHAPTER 11

Olli had never been kissed by a man like Spur. He didn't rush, though her pulse was frantic in her chest. He held her right where he wanted her, and she almost wanted those hands to wander a little bit. Hers did, up the sides of his face and into his hair. Down his neck to those beautiful shoulders.

He took his time, and Olli had no idea how long had passed before he finally broke their connection. She felt like he'd kissed her so completely that she'd never have need to kiss another man again.

She swayed on her feet, her eyes still closed, and Spur hung onto her hips, saying, "Whoa, there, Olli."

She opened her eyes then and met his. The moment between them felt tense, and a good laugh would break that ice. Olli didn't feel like laughing though. Her eyes dropped to his mouth again, and she tipped up onto her toes to touch her lips to his one more time.

This kiss didn't last nearly as long, and Olli pulled away first. "I really don't have anything for dinner," she said.

"I said I can order in," he said quietly. He made no move to get his phone out. "What do you want?"

"I don't know." She pressed her forehead to his collarbone, thinking maybe she should just get out a frozen pizza and call it good. Irritation ran through her that she couldn't seem to have one normal, romantic date with Spur. "My cat literally never comes out when people are here," she said. "Not even me."

"The call of the fish must've been too strong for him." Spur grinned at her and finally removed one hand from her waist to get his phone. "What about pasta and salad?" He looked at her, his eyebrows up.

"Sure," she said. "As long as it's from Wild Bikini."

He chuckled and tapped. "They're here. Thirty-seven minutes for delivery. That okay?" He looked to her for permission again, and Olli gave it.

"I want the diablo sauce with all the veggies over spaghetti."

"Okay," he said, his face taking on an air of concentration as he put in their order. "Olives?"

"Yes," she said.

He tapped a few more times and looked up. "It's on its way." He looked around her house, and Olli had wondered how long it would take him to realized she was burning her Get Your Man candles.

Turned out that Spur was ultra-observant. She knew the

moment he saw the flames flickering from no less than four candles, and he swallowed as he looked back at her.

"Only seven seconds," she said. "I think you get bonus points for that."

"Seven seconds for what?" he asked.

"To notice I've got all the candles burning."

Another swallow, which Olli found so cute. "Yeah," he said. "I see that."

She tried to step past him, but he hooked his arm around her waist and pulled her flush against him again. "What can I use my bonus points for?"

Olli looked up at him, liking the sparkle of flirtation in his eyes. "You seem to make up what you want to use them for, Mister Chappell," she said. "You tell me."

"I was thinking maybe a little of this." He dipped his head and ran his lips along her neck.

"Yeah," she said, breathless. "That's going to cost you a lot of points."

He chuckled and stepped back. "I'll stop then. I don't want to use all my points up tonight."

Heat ran through Olli from head to toe, but she managed to step over to the counter—her original destination. "Are you willing to be my sniffer until the food gets here?" She picked up the cologne cards she'd been working on for the past several days.

"Yep," he said, loosening that tie around his neck. "Let me get set up." He rolled his shoulders like he was going to be lifting some serious weights, and Olli giggled at him. He could make denim look like a million bucks, and she wondered how he did that.

He bent and picked up his cowboy hat from the floor, then did a few more toe-touches before he sat on the barstool and faced her. "Ready."

"You're adorable," she said, unable to wipe the smile from her face.

Spur scoffed. "No man wants to be called adorable. I hope that's not one of your scents."

"I do have a Baby Girl candle," Olli said without missing a beat. "It has Adorable in it."

Spur grinned at her and shook his head. "You're just digging a bigger hole for yourself, Olivia."

She burst out laughing and put her hand on his shoulder as if she needed him to steady herself. "I'll have to use some of my bonus points to get out," she said, quieting. "How many do I have left?"

"Probably fifty or so."

"Probably?"

They grinned at one another, and Olli took a moment to really appreciate him. It had only been a week since the sheep incident and their first date at Six Stars, but she'd known Spur Chappell for a lot longer than that.

"How many points do I have?" Spur asked, reaching out and trailing his fingers along hers.

"Seventy-four," she said, making up a number on the spot. "You'll earn some more with this smell-test." She looked down at her cards, which she'd marked with numbers. The scents were in a notebook in the perfumery. "Okay, here we go. Number one."

She held the card up, and he leaned forward to take a big breath of it. "Yeah, I actually like that one," he said. "It's nice and clean. A man always wants to smell clean when he goes out."

"Hmm," Olli said. "What else?"

"It's not blue," he said thoughtfully, and a flicker of surprise made Olli blink. He was a quick study, this cowboy. "It feels more...sunny. It has warmth in it. So it's clean, but it's also warm. Like maybe Sunshine?"

"It's actually Meadow," she said. "But I'm super impressed."

"Which is what?" he asked.

"Meadow is a bit of grass and a bit of light." Their eyes met, and she smiled at him. "It's a completely warm scent. Did you get anything else?"

"You always put something at the very bottom," he said. "It's the kicker. It's what makes someone want to buy the candle or the perfume, and they can hardly ever name it."

"Ten bonus points." Flirting with him was so much fun.

"I'm going to guess something masculine...clove?"

"At least you didn't say pine."

"I was listening the other night."

"Clearly." She put the card down, thrilled that he actively participated when they were together, even if the activity couldn't be all that fun for him. "It's not clove. It's frankincense, so you were very close."

She lifted another card, and they continued the smell-test.

She grabbed a pen after the second one and took notes, feeling like she was miles closer to achieving her men's line of scents and getting her grant.

They'd finished by the time the pasta arrived, and as Olli plated it up and served him at her clean dining room table, she asked, "Do you think there's anything we need to go over for the investor?"

"Maybe his name," Spur said, putting his napkin in his lap. "You haven't even told me that. Or much about the grant." He looked at her, and his eyes glinted in the candlelight between them.

"His name is Frank Renlund," she said. "He owns this *massive* consumer goods company. They make soaps and lotions, but also cleaners and even household products like paper towels and toasters and all of it."

"Wow," he said.

"Yeah." Olli looked down at her spicy pasta, her mouth watering but her nerves preventing her from taking a bite just yet. "Those who get a grant from him almost always get store placement too." She looked at Spur, needing him to understand how important this Saturday was to her. "I just learned that when his assistant called today."

"That's amazing," Spur said.

"They have over four hundred stores nation-wide," Olli said. The stakes for getting this grant felt so sharp and like they'd suddenly driven right into her soul. "I *need* to get this grant."

"You will," Spur said with all the confidence in the world.

He went back to his food and then looked at her again. "You're worried about it."

"Of course I am." Olli pushed her veggies around in the sauce, the scent of tomatoes and corn and cayenne meeting her nose. "It's just..." She sighed. "You don't get it, because you're rich. This is a *huge* opportunity for me. He chooses five small businesses to invest in every year, and his money could take Fluency to the next level."

"Fluency?"

"That's the name of my company," Olli said. She couldn't believe she hadn't told him that. What else had she failed to mention that Frank Renlund would expect her boyfriend to know?

"Oh, right," he said. "I saw that on the labels in the perfumery." He smiled at her, clearly not concerned. It faltered though, and he put his fork down. "Olli, what are you really worried about?"

"Just everything," she said. "I'm good with people, but I don't know what to expect. I've never hosted a CEO before." She couldn't look at him, because her insecurities weighed on her and kept her gaze on the table in front of her.

"What do you need help with?" he asked, threading his fingers through hers. She looked at the difference between her hands and his. His skin was darker, rougher, and yet so wonderful.

"I'm having Charity do all of the orders this week," Olli said. "I really want to have something to show Mister Renlund for the men's line, so he'll know what I'm going to use his money for. I develop three new scents per quarter too, and those cost a lot in terms of time and money—growing product —all of it, and I want to show him the things I'm rolling out in July, August, and September. The last one is almost done."

He let a few seconds of silence go by, and Olli finally looked at him. His eyes were wide, thoughtful, and caring. "Anything I can do to help?"

"I need to clean up the perfumery too," she said. "Big time."

"I can do that," he said. "Your new honeysuckle will be here tomorrow. I'll make sure that goes in."

"I'm getting gladiolus tomorrow too," she said.

"I can plant them," he said.

"Bonus points for knowing it was a flower."

Their eyes met again, and this time, Spur leaned toward her, his intent clear. She went the rest of the distance and kissed him. His lips trembled slightly, and he kept the kiss sweet. With that single kiss, he burrowed straight into her heart, and when he pulled away and said, "I'll help you, Olli. It's going to be great, you'll see," she thought she fell a little bit in love with him.

She instinctively reached for something to grab onto, because falling always hurt. She looked at Spur and finally got a taste of her diablo sauce, deciding that if he was at the bottom of the cliff to catch her, she might be okay with the falling.

CHAPTER 12

Blaine Chappell left the meeting in a worse mood than when he'd gone in. One of their pastures definitely needed to be vacated of all cattle and burned. Spur would not be happy about that. Heck, Blaine wasn't happy about it, because he was the one who had to deal with the infected animals, the veterinarians, the concerned trainers, the scheduling of treatments, and so much more.

His head hurt, and he hated that his phone kept chiming. *Ding, ding, ding.* He wanted to throw the stupid thing into the nearest compost pile and get a new number.

He shook the thoughts from his head, because they weren't entirely true. He loved getting messages from his best friend, Tamara Lennox. She always sent him a lot of messages on Mondays, because it was her day to be in the saddle shop, and she took a ton of pictures, texted them to him, and asked his advice.

He'd known her for over two decades now, as she'd moved to Dreamsville as a Freshman, and the town wasn't all that big. She loved horses as much as any Chappell, and she was always willing to come out to the ranch to help when Blaine needed it.

He definitely needed her now, and he ducked around the corner to read her messages.

Today, she'd sent several saddles, as usual. She got excited when she got new leather, and Blaine felt some of his bad mood lift with her excitement over the cow hide leather she'd received in her workshop that day.

She also bought finished leathers from overseas, and the beautiful, dark chestnut piece in the next picture would make a beautiful saddlebag. Tam was a master at making things out of leather, and she understood what cowboys wanted. She sold saddles all over the South, into Texas, and up into Montana and Canada.

Amazing, he sent back to her. His fingers flew as he transitioned the conversation from her leather goods to his ranch problems. *I'm wondering if you can come help me at the ranch tonight. There's this problem with—*

He stopped as her next message came in. "No," he said, the word coming without him thinking about it.

Guess who's coming back into town next month? Hayes.

Blaine did not like Hayes Powell, mostly because he'd taken Tam's heart straight from her chest and crushed it in his bare hands. He'd never seen Tam cry—until Hayes had broken their engagement and left town. She was a tough woman, and she'd ridden the rodeo circuit, broken bones, and lost her grandmother to cancer—all tear-free.

Blaine frowned as he first erased his message and then tapped to call Tam.

"I knew you'd call," she said.

"Why is he coming back?"

"I guess his dad is sick." Tam sighed, and Blaine could see her tucking her nearly white-blonde hair behind her ear as she did. "I'm not going to go back to him."

"Of course you're not," Blaine said. He couldn't help wondering why he and Tam had never tried a relationship, but he pushed the idea out of his head. He'd ended his own engagement once, and while Tam had been very supportive of his decision, when her own had ended, she'd told him she sincerely hoped his fiancée didn't feel like she did.

Things hadn't quite been the same between them since. Sometimes Blaine thought Tam assumed that his ex-fiancée felt the way she had when Hayes had ended their relationship.

Blaine knew that wasn't true, but he'd never told Tam that his ex had been cheating on him. No man wanted to admit that, and he'd only told Spur and Trey. He definitely knew he hadn't broken Alex's heart the way Hayes had shattered Tam's.

"I just...I need him to know I'm over him," Tam said.

"Why does it matter?" Blaine asked. What he really wanted to ask was if Tam was over Hayes or not. Their wedding would've been last June, so almost a year had passed since then. He'd broken up with her two months before that, and Blaine realized he'd missed the anniversary of it. Tam hadn't said anything either, so she probably was over Hayes.

She wasn't dating anyone else, though, and she hadn't since the break-up.

"Think about Hayes for a second," Tam said dryly, and while Blaine would rather not think about the man, he did.

He'd known Hayes for several years too. Anyone working in the racehorse industry knew each other, and Hayes had been a starting gate trainer. Every horse that touched the track at a nearby facility went through him to learn how to deal with the starting gate. He'd been very good at his job, and he knew it.

He knew he was handsome. He knew he had a great laugh, and a perfectly symmetrical smile. Blaine had seen him get the numbers from four different women in one evening during a gala for people in the industry.

He was arrogant and tall, and he seemed to know exactly how to get Tam to bend to his every wish and desire.

Blaine's throat closed as he frowned. "You're not even going to talk to him, Tam. Promise me."

"If I had a boyfriend, he wouldn't even approach me," she said.

"Get a boyfriend, then."

"You make it sound so easy, like I can just walk into the Finn's and pick one up off the shelf."

Blaine looked down the aisle, wishing a solution would present itself. "Yeah, I get it's not that easy."

"Yeah, or else you'd have a girlfriend," she said, her voice lightening a little.

"I doubt it," he said.

"Listen, I have to run, but I don't want you to worry about this. I'm not going to talk to him."

"I'm already worrying about it," Blaine said, blinking to get his focus back. "Can you come help me tonight? I can text you the details."

"Sure," she said. "We can talk more then about my getting-a-boyfriend strategy." She laughed, but Blaine knew she did that to cover up awkward moments.

He chuckled anyway and said, "Okay, come by whenever you can. If I'm not in the front shed, I'll be at the house."

"Okay, bye." Just like that, she was gone.

Blaine stayed where he was, his mind moving through the numerous things he needed to do before Tam showed up that night. He didn't want to talk to Spur, because he was already dealing with some hard things. He could save that conversation for their morning meeting tomorrow.

"Start with Harmon," he said, pushing away from the wall. Harmon Hall was the field manager, and he'd be able to tell Blaine which pastures they could move the cattle into so they could purge the infected field and get the hoof rot off the ranch.

Blaine picked up the last piece of his peanut butter sandwich and popped it into his mouth. He didn't mind eating sandwiches and chips for dinner, though he had some pickier brothers. Conrad refused to eat anything but a hot meal for both lunch and dinner, and he was definitely the biggest diva when it came to his food.

Blaine was fine with bread and peanut butter, and he kept a stash of both in the front shed. He operated from there a lot of the time, so he wasn't in the way in the stables, row houses, or training facilities. He did a ton of work with the racehorses the family actually owned, but Spur kept up with them too, as did all of the brothers. They each managed something to do with the champion horses they raised, and Blaine's contribution was to monitor their health as they grew into the running powerhouses they all wanted them to be.

The Chappells didn't make much money on horses that couldn't run, and a healthy horse trained faster and better than an unhealthy one.

He finished putting together his plan for his meeting with Spur in the morning, realizing that Tam hadn't stopped by yet. A quick glance at his phone told him it was past eight, and that was pretty late for her to not be done with her work.

He picked up his phone at the same time a text from her arrived. They'd joked in the past about how she could tell if he was thinking about her, and he could tell if she was talking about him. A smile crossed his face as he read her message.

I can practically hear you wondering where I am. I'm just leaving. Be there in ten.

Great, he said, neither confirming nor denying that he'd been thinking about her. She wouldn't believe him if he denied it anyway. *Meet me around the northwest side*, he typed out. *I'm headed to the pasture there.*

She didn't confirm, because Tam was super strict about not texting while she drove. Her mother had been in a car accident about five years ago, caused by someone texting and not seeing the red light. They'd ran it and hit her mother. She'd made a complete recovery, but once Tam seized onto something, she didn't let it go very easily.

He rode an ATV over to the northwest side of the ranch and parked beside the pasture they'd be vacating in the morning. He had Harmon ready to go, along with his crew of three cowboys. If Blaine could get Tam to come, they could move the cattle all at once, in under an hour.

Then he could take her to lunch and ask her if she wanted him to be her boyfriend.

A sigh escaped from his mouth, because the unsettling thought was just there in his mind. It had been popping up all day too, and he couldn't help the way he felt about her.

"You don't like her," he muttered. "At least not for more than your best friend. You're just worried about her."

He was just being overprotective. *Mothering*, Trey called it. Blaine had taken the teasing from his next oldest brother, because he couldn't really argue with him. Blaine was the most "mothering" of all the Chappell men. He couldn't help it if he wanted everyone to have what they needed to be happy, and his own mother had told him never to apologize for thinking about and caring about others.

"It's your dear heart that makes you amazing," she'd told him once.

She didn't think he was all that amazing now, especially

after he'd ended things with Alex. His mother had *loved* Alex, as they both served on a fundraising committee to rescue mistreated horses. They'd gone to lunches and events together, and as far as Blaine knew, they still did. The difference was, he didn't have to hear about them. He didn't have to smell another man's cologne on Alex's skin when she returned from an event. He didn't have to listen to her lie and then stay awake at night and wonder what to do.

Yes, he'd taken control of his life, and he was doing just fine.

"Better than fine," he said to the cows in the distance. "I'm happy. I know who I am, and I'm happy."

"That makes one of us."

Blaine yelped at the addition of another voice to his solace. He leapt right, away from the sound and looked at the woman who'd arrived.

Tam had her wavy hair pulled up into a ponytail, and she wore jeans, boots, and a sleeveless shirt the color of ripe peaches. "I love it when you talk to yourself," she teased.

"How are you so silent when you move?" He turned and found her truck parked several yards away, and he should've been able to hear that thing arrive. It was easily fifteen years old, and the engine growled every time she started it.

"I'm a ninja." She laughed and put her foot up on the rung, a sigh leaking out of her mouth. Several seconds passed, and Blaine's pulse settled back into a normal rhythm. "I'm glad you're happy, Blaine."

"Thanks," he said. "What can we do to make you happy?"

"Not possible." She lifted one shoulder in a shrug, and

Blaine stared at her creamy skin. Just as quickly as he'd fallen into the stare, he yanked his eyes away. He was *not* interested in Tam, not romantically.

"Come on," he said. "You seemed happy about that Italian leather."

"It's actually from the bulls in Barcelona," she said, shooting him a grin.

"Oh, okay, Ms. Know-It-All."

They laughed, and everything aligned regarding Tam. Thankfully. Blaine didn't want to think about her as girlfriend material, because it complicated so much.

"Hoof rot, huh?" she asked.

"Yes," he said. "If you can come tomorrow around ten, we can move the cattle in one herd. We treated them once this afternoon, and we will again in the morning. Then I've got the Fire Marshall coming to do a controlled burn of the field."

"Won't you just have to burn the pasture you put them in?"

"No, because they've already started treatment."

She nodded. "I can come at ten, but I want to ride Florence Nightingale, *and* I need something from you."

"Flo is ready for you," he said. "You act like I don't know what you'll need to come do my dirty work." He nudged her with his elbow.

She grinned at him and leaned her head against his shoulder. "You're the best, Blaine."

"I know I am." They looked out over the pasture together, and contentment moved through Blaine. He certainly did not want to ruin that by trying to be Tam's boyfriend. "What did you need from me?"

"You're not going to like it."

His heartbeat jumped. "Spit it out."

"I've got a friend who needs a date for a wedding..." she started.

"No," Blaine said, his voice hard.

"I'm going to be there," Tam said. "It'll be fine. She just —she used to date the groom, and she can't show up alone."

Blaine's jaw tightened as his teeth pressed together. "What is with you guys? Why can't she go alone? Or better yet—don't go at all."

"She can't do that," Tam said.

"Women are very complicated."

"It's three hours," she said. "You'll get steak and lobster, if that makes you feel better. Cake too."

"Trying to win me over with food never works, Tam. You know that."

"It was worth a try." She linked her arm through his, and Blaine's blood heated. Why was it doing that? He'd never felt anything for Tam before. He was just all over the place today. "I really do need a boyfriend for when Hayes comes back, though."

"I don't see why," Blaine said, having had the chance to think about the situation and prepare his argument. "You're smart and successful, Tam. You don't need him. Why would you think you wouldn't be able to resist his not-that-charm-ing-personality?"

"I don't know," she said, her voice on the low end of her range.

"I don't understand why you'd go back to someone who made you feel so terrible about yourself, even if he did show up with your favorite daisies and say how sorry he was. He should have to do all of that and then prove it for the next five years before you even *think* about taking him back."

"I don't want him back," she said, shooting him a glare.

"Then why do you need a boyfriend?"

"Maybe I don't want to be alone anymore," she said, her tone laced with anger now. "Have you thought of that, Blaine? That sure, I can be smart and successful, but at the end of the day, I go home alone."

Blaine didn't know what to say next. She edged away from him, and he felt like the ocean now separated them. "I'm sorry," he said.

"You just don't get it, because you *like* being alone."

"Is that what you think?"

"Why don't you date?" She faced him then, her bright blue eyes full of challenge. There was still plenty of sunlight left to see everything on her face too. "You know it's hard for women to get dates. They can't *really* ask a man without coming off as desperate. And yet, *you're* not asking anyone to go out with you. None of you Chappells do."

"That's just not true," Blaine said, his own fire really getting stoked now. "Conrad and Duke have girlfriends. Spur does now too." He looked down to her work boots and back to her face. "Are you saying you want one of us to ask you out? Who? I'll talk to him."

She rolled her eyes and faced the field again. "I don't want to go out with one of your brothers."

"Are you sure? Because it sounded like you did."

"I don't." She practically bit the words out of her mouth.

Blaine sighed and looked out at the pasture too. He didn't want to tell her everything, but maybe he'd carried it for long enough. "I don't date, Tam, because I don't want to get hurt again."

"What do you mean?"

"I mean, I broke off my engagement with Alex, because she was cheating on me." There. He'd said it.

"She was not." Tam sounded horrified, and when Blaine looked at her, he found her eyes wide and her mouth hanging open. "Why would anyone do that?"

"Because she's not a nice person?" He shrugged. "I'm over her. I am. I'm just maybe not ready to let someone new in yet."

"I'm sorry, Blaine," she said, linking her arm through his again and leaning her head against his shoulder. "I didn't know."

"Assumptions aren't pleasant," he said, repeating something his father had told him many times.

She nodded, and they fell into silence. Blaine had always been so comfortable with Tam, and he didn't want to lose that. Deep down, he didn't want her to date anyone, because if she fell in love and got married, they couldn't be best friends anymore. He wouldn't want his wife to be snuggled up with another man, talking about life and love and everything in between.

"I have an idea," Tam said, and Blaine looked at her as she straightened.

"Oh, no," he said, finding that mischievous glint in those baby blues. "I've seen that look before, and I almost got arrested when I went along with your idea."

"Just hear me out," she said, but she simply stood there and looked at him, not saying anything.

CHAPTER 13

Tamara Lennox couldn't believe what she was about to propose.

Bad word choice, she told herself, her voice still not working. She'd been friends with Blaine since the moment they met. They were just two peas in a pod, cut from the same cloth, and born with the same eyes.

That was what her mother said, anyway.

She'd always gotten along with him, and some of her best memories included him.

Why shouldn't she include him when she needed him most?

"Are you going to say anything?" he asked. "Or am I supposed to guess what your idea is?" He folded his arms, and the man had some impressive muscles. He liked to lift weights in the shed where he worked, and Tam suddenly wanted to see how heavy the barbells were.

She cleared her throat. "Yes, I'm going to say something."

"Spit it out," he said again, looking out across the field. He seemed off, but Tam couldn't put her finger on exactly how. She'd always been able to tell when something was bothering Blaine Chappell, and something was definitely bothering him.

"I think you should be my boyfriend," she said, spitting it all out at once, just like ripping off a bandage.

He turned toward her, his eyes wide. He had eyes the color of coffee with a lot of cream in them, and she'd always found them beautiful. She'd seen them dance when he laughed and water when he cried. She'd seen a glint of naughtiness in them in the past, and plenty of happiness or contentment as he simply lived his life.

"Excuse me?" he asked, reaching up to press down on his cowboy hat. He never went anywhere without that thing, and Tam knew better than to try to remove it from his head. She'd thought that would be a funny joke, but Blaine had disagreed. She'd learned that day never to touch a man's cowboy hat unless she felt like losing a limb.

"You and me," she said, rushing still. "It would be perfect. Hayes wouldn't know the difference, because he was always saying you were getting in between us. He seriously thought we were having a fling on the side." She knew she wasn't winning him over, but she pressed on. "You could then get back out in the dating game. We go to dinner, women see you're available and willing, and bam, when we break-up—after Hayes leaves town—you're back on the market. It'll be easy for you to get a date."

He cocked his hip and squinted his eyes. With the folded arms, and the cowboy hat, he really had the disgusted, *are-you-*

kidding-me look down just right. "This is a joke, right?" he asked.

"It's not a joke," she said, playfully pushing against his chest. He didn't move an inch. "It's an *idea*."

"It's a bad idea," he grumbled, turning back to the ATV he'd obviously ridden out here.

"Why?" she asked. "You find me so disgusting you couldn't hold my hand through a movie?"

"No," he said.

"You hate my hair," she said next. "It *has* been frizzing out a lot lately."

He rolled his eyes, but he didn't deny that her hair was too frizzy. She'd curled it that day, and that seemed to tame some of the poof.

"We won't have to kiss or anything," she said, watching him closely. She'd thought about kissing Blaine plenty of times in the past. She'd entertained a crush on the teenager for a full year, until he graduated, and she stayed in high school. Then again once she finished the farrier program and then a leather-working course, specifically for making saddles. She'd returned to Dreamsville then, and Blaine was back in town too. He'd taken a few college courses but hadn't graduated.

He didn't need a degree to work on his family's prestigious ranch and inherit a ton of money. Just how much, he'd never told her. He had a lot of brothers, and the most he'd said was, "It's a lot, Tam. For all of us."

"You said you didn't want to let in someone new," she said. "I'm not new."

"These are really bad arguments," he said.

"You wouldn't even be letting me in. *I'm* already in." She would never hurt him. "How hard can it be? We hold hands and go to dinner. We practically do that anyway."

"We do not," he said.

"I just had my arm laced through yours." She mimicked him by cocking her hip and folding her arms. "We stand out here and watch the sun go down. Anyone passing by would think we were together."

He looked at her then, and she saw the idea bubbling and brewing in his mind. Victory was close, and Tam just needed to close the deal.

"You definitely won't get arrested for dating me," she said. "It only has to *look* like dating on the outside." She'd wanted him to ask her out on her thirtieth birthday too. They'd once made a pact with each other that if they didn't have a significant other on her thirtieth birthday, he'd ask her out.

He'd obviously forgotten, because she'd gotten a deluxe set of mats for her car instead of an invitation to dinner. She'd said nothing, because Blaine obviously wasn't interested in her romantically, just like he wasn't now.

He was, however, her best friend, and she knew he'd do anything for her.

"I'll plan everything," she said. "I'll pay for all of it. All you have to do is show up and look pretty on my arm."

"I am not pretty," he growled.

She laughed, because he sure was fun to tease. Cute when he was mad too, and Tam found herself crushing on him all over again. Her feelings seemed to resurface every five years or so, and that meant they were right on time.

When he didn't relent with the glaring, she switched tactics. She issued a long sigh from her mouth and started back toward her truck. "All right," she said. "You win. It was a bad idea." She paused next to the quad. "I still have a few more weeks until Hayes comes into town. I'll find someone else."

She smiled and said, "See you in the morning," before turning and walking away.

She'd just reached for the door handle on her nearly broken-down truck when he said, "Tam, wait."

She turned her head toward him and waited.

"How are you going to find someone else?" he asked.

He might as well have played right into her hand. She shrugged and looked away. "Dating app. Or that hook-up website."

"No," he practically barked. His footsteps sounded loud as he marched toward her. "You can't get on that website. I forbid it."

"You forbid it?" She grinned up at him, noting that he'd moved in quite close to her. "You're not my father, Blaine. I need someone for this, and those two places are the best ones to find men willing to go along with a little charade for like, a week." She knew it would be more than a week; Blaine did too. If Hayes's father was really ill, he could be back in town for a while.

He'd left to work with a specific horse and training crew in California. It had been a great opportunity for him. Tam was supposed to go with him; they were to be married. She could go anywhere with him.

He'd said right to her face he didn't want her to come. He

didn't want her.

The same ice that had flushed through her system then threatened to do so now. Blaine didn't want her either. Would anyone ever want her?

"Let me think about it," Blaine said, and Tam felt the hook lodge in his throat. Now all she had to do was reel him in.

"How about this?" she asked. "You think about it. You make your list of rules like you like to do. We'll go to dinner this weekend, and you can present them to me." She grinned at him. "Okay?"

"You think you have everything figured out," he said, his voice vicious but a smile touching his mouth too.

She laughed again, glad when he let the smile out and shook his head. "Blaine, baby, when it comes to you, I *do* have everything figured out."

"I think you've forgotten that I know you as well as you know me."

Tam sobered, because if that were true, he'd know how she felt about him. How she'd felt about him *in the past*.

"We'll meet at Mindie's," he said. "Friday. Six-thirty. You'll order the fried calamari, and I'll get the appetizer medley with the cheesy garlic knots. I'll lay out the rules, and you'll tell me I owe you because of all the work you do around here for me."

"See?" she asked, slipping back into a flirty and innocent space. It was far too hard to exist in the spot where she wanted him and he didn't even see her. "You have everything figured out too." She opened her truck door and climbed behind the wheel. "See you in the morning *and* on Friday night."

Tam wanted to stay and talk more with Blaine. Or just stand next to him. She wanted to ask him what was really wrong and share an intimate moment with him where he told her things he'd never told anyone else. She couldn't, though, because it was too dangerous.

She started the truck, which caused Blaine to jump backward like the vehicle might consume him if he stayed too close. She waved, her plastic smile plastered on her face, and she left Bluegrass Ranch.

"It's better this way," she said as the smile slipped from her face. *I know who I am, and I'm happy.*

Blaine's words ran through her mind as she drove home, which was only a half a mile as the crow flies from the ranch. She wished she knew who she was, and she wished she were happy.

She parked in her driveway and went up the front steps, getting rushed by two overeager corgis the moment she went inside. "Hey, guys," she said, laughing at them as they jumped up on her legs. "You're happy to see me, right? Yes, you are. Yes, I'm happy to see you, too."

She was happy to see her dogs. She loved her job. She had friends.

She straightened and looked around the semi-dark house. No matter how many things made her happy, she still had to come home to a husbandless house. A distinct thread of *un*happiness moved through her, and she hated that she wanted to be married so badly.

Plenty of women didn't need a man to be happy. Tam just wished she was one of them.

CHAPTER 14

S pur didn't particularly enjoy gardening, but he had a debt to pay and pay it he would. The sun burned hotly overhead as he got the honeysuckle planted. He stood and stretched his back, a groan coming out of his mouth.

Olli had not made an appearance yet that morning, though the gladiolus she'd ordered stood over on the sidewalk, waiting for him to get them in the ground too.

His phone rang before he could take a step toward them, and Spur stared at the word *Mom* on the screen. He didn't really want to talk to her yet, but he supposed it had been a few days since the picnic.

"Hey," he said. "What's up, Ma?"

"Good morning," she chirped. "I came to see if you had time for lunch today, but Cayden says you're not even on the ranch."

"I'm repairing some damage our sheep did," he said, being

careful not to say anything like, *I'm at Olli's,* or *I'm helping Olli.*

He hadn't lied either. He probably should've said a prayer before answering a call from his mother, but there hadn't been time. He wiped the sweat from his forehead and waited for his mom to get to the point.

"Your father and I would like to have dinner with you and Olli."

Spur hated any sentence that came from his mother that started "Your father and I." Daddy did it too, and Spur really wished they'd just speak for themselves.

"I don't think so, Mom."

"Why not?"

"Because I've only been seeing her for a week. I don't think we're to that stage where I take her home to meet my parents yet."

"You brought her to the picnic."

"No," Spur said. "I invited her to come, and thankfully, she didn't break-up with me over how insane everyone is."

"Is this serious?" his mom asked.

"Did you hear the part where I said I've been seeing her for a week?" Spur gazed at the land in the distance, easily picking out the features on the ranch he knew so well. "Mom, I don't think you should get your hopes up, okay? We're just friends. I'm helping her with an investment." That should get her off his back for a while. He could circle back to it once things with Olli did turn serious.

"Spur," his mother said, her voice stern now. "Tell me you're not giving her money."

"No, Ma." He sighed and wiped his face again. "I'm not giving her money." That might be easier than winning over Frank Renlund though.

"Some women will do anything to get money," his mother said.

Spur knew that. Not as well as Ian, but well enough. "We're just having a good time, Ma." He sighed and turned around, coming face-to-face with Olli. He sucked in a breath, his mind racing.

How much had she heard?

Enough, judging by the sharpness in her eyes and the snarl on her lips. She carried two cups of coffee, and she cocked her eyebrows at him as she deliberately turned one upside down and poured it out.

He jumped back as the hot coffee splashed his boots, and said, "Olli, just a second," as she stormed away from him. "I'll call you back, Mom." He hung up and shoved his phone in his back pocket, calling, "Olli, wait," again.

She did not wait, and she could move fast when she wanted to. She went up the front steps to her porch and straight inside before Spur had even reached the sidewalk.

"Stupid," he said to himself, still intent on going after her. He reached the door and tried the knob, but it was locked. He pounded on the door with an open palm. "Olli, come on," he said.

The door flew inward as she yanked it open. "We're just friends?"

Spur opened his mouth to respond, but she held up her hand.

"You're just helping me," she said. "We're just having a good time."

He did not like the sarcastic tone in her voice.

"Some women will do anything for money." She could've cut holes straight through him with her disgust. "Don't get your hopes up."

He wasn't sure if she was finished or not, and Spur had learned to let a woman say what was on her mind before he tried to explain.

She scoffed, rolled her eyes, and slammed the door in his face. He flinched as the lock clicked, and helplessness drove through him. "Olli," he called again. "Let me explain."

"Go ahead," she yelled from inside. "Explain, O Mighty Spur."

Frustration filled him, and Spur didn't want to yell through the door. He also didn't think she'd actually hear a word he said in the emotional state she was in.

He backed away from the door and took a seat on the top step. *I'm sorry*, he sent to her. *Just come outside when you're ready, and I'll explain everything.*

He had plenty to do back on the ranch today, but he was willing to sit there all day if he had to. Blaine had the hoof rot under control, and Spur expected to see smoke in the sky by lunchtime. He used to get upset about diseases and the setbacks they caused. But he'd learned over the years that he should expect such things. They were going to happen whether he got mad about them or not. No one could prevent everything, all the time.

Only five minutes later, the door behind him opened.

Spur scrambled to his feet and swiped his cowboy hat off his head. "I'm sorry," he said aloud, deciding to lead the discussion this time. "It was just my mother, and you don't know her real well yet, but I know how to handle her."

"By lying to her?"

"She just makes such a big deal out of everything," Spur said, desperate for Olli to understand. "We *are* new, Olli, and yeah, maybe I said we were just having a good time when we're not, but I don't know. I'm having a good time."

"You know what that means, though, right?"

"Yes," he said, hanging his head.

"You said you were too old to play games."

"I am."

"Then why can't you just tell her the truth?"

"You don't know her." He looked up at Olli, who clearly didn't believe him. "I'll talk to her this afternoon. She invited us for dinner with her and my dad, like I'm going to be proposing to you by the weekend." How could he help her see? "Once, when Blaine was dating this woman, he went to the parent dinner. My mother actually asked his girlfriend what size she was and if she'd consider getting married at the country club so we wouldn't have to have so many people out to the ranch. Needless to say, she broke up with Blaine that very night. They'd been out four times."

Olli started to soften, and Spur didn't want to throw his mother under the bus. He loved her; he did. She had moments where she was wonderful, and he appreciated all his parents had done for him, all they'd provided so he could have the life he did.

"I told her what would get her off my back," he said. "I was actually trying to protect you."

"You want to protect yourself," she said.

"That too," he admitted. He took one step forward, buoyed when she didn't retreat from him. "Please don't be mad."

"Tell me the truth," she said. "Don't hold back, Spur. I'm a big girl. I can take it."

"You want the truth?" He swallowed, unsure of what she required of him.

"Yes," she said.

He licked his lips, and he saw no way out of saying what was in his heart. "The truth, Olli, is that I've already started to fall in love with you. I think you're sexy, and smart, and resourceful. I think you're tenacious in the best way possible. I love spending time with you, and I've started to imagine what life would be like with you at my side all the time." He swallowed again, his throat so dry and so narrow. "I'm *not* here just for a good time. We're *way* more than friends. I am helping you with an investment, and I'd give you the money you needed if you'd accept it from me." He twisted his hat, running his fingers along the outside of the brim, trying to find anything else to say.

"I think that's it," he said, nodding. "That's the truth."

She sized him up, and Spur stood very still while she did. "Okay," she finally said.

"Okay?" he repeated.

"Yeah, okay." She reached for him, and he twined his fingers through hers.

"Can I kiss you to make sure we're okay?" he asked, crowding into her personal space.

"If you must," she said with a sigh, and Spur chuckled as he pressed his cowboy hat to her back and kissed her. "See?" he whispered, his lips catching on hers. "Way more than friends." He kissed her again, feeling her melt into him. He sure did like that, and Spur hoped she could also feel the truth of what he'd said.

"Yeah," she said, breaking their connection. "I don't want your money, Spur. You know that's not why I asked you to help me, right?"

"I know that." He held her close to his chest, despite the heat. "Why did you ask me?"

"You trampled my flowers."

"So if Cayden had done that, or Ian, or Conrad, you'd have asked them?" He pulled away and looked at her. Anxiety ran through her expression, and Spur thought he had the answer.

"No," she said. "I've always known you the best, Spur. I would've asked you without the sheep incident."

"Yeah? You know there's a website to get dates for a party or a wedding or whatever."

"Have you used that site?" she asked, plenty of incredulity in her voice.

"No, I've just heard about it."

"It's a creeper site," she said. "Women should not be using it."

Spur didn't really know what that meant, so he said nothing. She would've asked him. She kissed him like they were way more than friends. He didn't need her to spell everything out for him the way he had for her.

"Is there any coffee left?" he asked, slinging his arm around her shoulders. "Are you gonna come help me with these gladiolus? I didn't ruin any of them, you know."

She smiled and tucked her hair behind her ear. "Yeah, I'll come help. Let's have coffee first."

* * *

Spur took a deep breath and offered up that prayer he'd considered that morning. Then he strode up the sidewalk to his parents' front door. His mother's hanging flower pots gave the air a fresh fragrance, something Spur would've never noticed before his relationship with Olli.

"Your relationship," he muttered to himself, still a little surprised he had a relationship with a woman.

He reached the door and opened it as he called, "Ma? Daddy?"

"On the upper verandah," his mother called, and Spur worked hard not to roll his eyes. It wouldn't matter if he did, though, as the "upper verandah" was just the back porch. He crossed through the small house to the open back door and stepped onto the lower deck. Several feet up sat the upper deck, and it got more shade at this time of day due to the huge trees on that side of the house.

"Hey." He climbed the steps and sat in an available chair. "How are you feeling, Daddy?"

"Good today," he said.

"He hasn't needed a painkiller since breakfast," Ma said, and Spur smiled.

"That's great." He leaned his forearms on his knees and looked at the ground. His cowboy boots were filthy, and he probably should've kicked them off by the front door.

"What brings you by?" his mother asked.

Spur looked up at her, his neck growing tired after only a moment. "Do you really want to know?"

"You came over," she said, lifting a glass of iced sweet tea to her lips.

"I know, but do you really want the truth?" He flicked his gaze to his father, who wore a resigned look. He wanted the truth, Spur knew.

"You're going to say what you want anyway," Mom said. "Just say it."

"I don't want to hurt your feelings," he said, because he genuinely didn't.

She finally looked at him, her eyes wide and full of vulnerability. "I'll let you know if I want you to stop."

Spur nodded, trying to organize the words in his mind. The hard conversations always fell to him. He'd been the one to show up at the house and tell his father that he had to get a hearing aid or he and the other brothers weren't going to let him go to auctions anymore.

He'd been the one to come to the house and tell his parents that Ian's wife had tried to steal from him. He'd been the one to come bearing the bad news that their prize horse, the one they'd invested hundreds of thousands of hours and dollars in, had fallen and broken a leg.

Somehow, telling them about Olli was just as hard.

"I have a couple of things," he said slowly. "First is Olli. I lied to you this morning, Ma, just to get you to stop bugging me."

"I was not bugging—"

"Let the man talk, honeybear," Daddy said, putting his hand on Mom's leg. She looked at him, surprise running through her expression. She nodded and took another gulp of her tea.

"You *do* bug me about women, Ma," Spur said quietly. "It doesn't help. It just pushes me further away and honestly, because of the Chappell stubborn streak, it makes me not want to date." He looked at her, hoping she'd see his love for her despite the hard things he was saying. "I'm not the only one who feels that way. Ian hasn't been out with anyone in five years, Ma. Cayden laughs when you say he let a good woman get away, but it cuts him all the way to the core."

No, none of his brothers had said much to him about this, but Spur had eyes. He knew what it was like to be the son of his mother and father. Actions always spoke louder than words anyway.

"Alex isn't a good woman, Ma," he said next. "Blaine hasn't told you the truth about why he ended their engagement, and if you were more approachable, he would."

She opened her mouth but promptly shut it again. She swiped at her eyes quickly and looked toward the big trees to her left.

"I'm sorry," Spur said, regret and true pain lancing through him. "I can be done."

"It's okay," she said. "I've heard this before from your father."

Spur met his father's eye, and he nodded a couple of times. His jaw was set, and Spur didn't expect him to say anything. He obviously had eyes too.

"Raising eight sons made your mother tough," Daddy said. "She's forgotten that she doesn't have eight rambunctious, naughty boys under age twelve anymore."

"I'm working on it," she said, still refusing to look at Spur.

"That's all we want, Ma," Spur said. "I'm forty-six years old, and yes, I'm dating Olivia Hudson. She's been right there all this time, and I guess I just didn't realize how I felt about her until we started seeing more of each other."

"That's great," Daddy said.

"I don't want to bring her to dinner until I'm more sure about things between us," he said, though he was pretty dang sure. "I sure do like her, and she seems to like me, but the fact is, it's been a week."

His mother nodded, and Spur added, "It's not a fling, and it's not me just having a good time. We're not just friends."

"I understand," she said, finally flicking a glance in his direction. "I won't ask you about her again. You can tell me what you want, when you want."

"Sounds good," Spur said, relief flooding him. "If you really mean that."

"I really mean it," she said.

"You won't press me for more details?" he asked. "You won't try to give me unsolicited advice?"

She looked at Daddy, and he squeezed her hand. She met

Spur's eye again, and she seemed one breath away from complete collapse. "Yes," she said. "I won't do either of those things."

Spur wasn't sure he believed her, but he supposed he could give her another chance. "Okay, great," he said. "Thanks, Mom."

"What's the second thing?" Daddy asked.

Spur frowned. "I think I said them both, all wrapped up in there. First, I wanted to set the record straight about me and Olli. And I wanted you guys to know that we love you, but man, you're hard to be around sometimes." He watched them for their reaction, gutted when his father dropped his eyes to his lap.

"You're both amazing parents," Spur said. "I know we weren't easy to raise, and Daddy, you ran the whole ranch too. I know you had to be tough and rough and never let anything slide more than a millimeter. But we really aren't invalids. We're not stupid. And we're not children anymore."

"I know," Daddy said. "I'm sorry I laughed when you said you were dating Olli. I was just surprised."

Spur nodded. "I get it. I haven't dated in years either." He didn't look at his mom. "I guess I just didn't realize how lonely I am."

"Spur," his mother said, her voice cracking.

"Don't cry, Ma," he said, getting up and bending down to hug her. "It's okay, I swear. I'll tell the others what you're trying to do, okay?"

She nodded against his shoulder and pulled back. She wiped her eyes quickly and set her shoulders to a perfect square. She really was tough. "Let them know we'd love to see them too," she said. "Anytime they want to come by the house."

Spur cocked his head. "They don't come by?" Spur made it a point to come every week, usually on Sundays.

"Not very often," Daddy said quietly. "We know we're not perfect, and we know the distance between us and you boys is our fault."

"It'll take all of us to heal the rift," Spur said. "I'll talk to them." He offered his parents a smile, and gave them each another hug before he said, "I have to go. I'm supposed to check in with Blaine before the sun sets."

He waved goodbye to them and headed out, his heart heavy with his father's regret, and filled with his mother's tears.

"Dear Lord," he said as he walked away from their house. "Bless us all to find the path toward a better time, with stronger family bonds." He didn't want to address this issue with his brothers, but he would, because he was the oldest, and he didn't want the cracks and fissures in his family to continue to widen.

CHAPTER 15

Olli helped Charity put the last candle into the final box. "Done," she said, passing it to her friend and employee, who taped it and peeled off the address label. "Thank you, Charity. You've worked so much this week."

"It's fine," the younger woman drawled. "School's out for the summer." She smiled prettily at Olli. "You don't need me until next week?"

"That's right," Olli said, looking around the perfumery. "Spur's coming to help me clean tonight. Tomorrow, Frank Renlund will be here, and whatever will be, will be." She sighed, her hopes so high she was sure they'd be shot down at least a little bit.

She'd seen Spur every night this week except for last night. He'd called a brothers-only dinner at the ranch, and he'd texted afterward that he was too tired to come sit on her back porch and look at the stars.

She hadn't heard from him today at all, and Olli's insecurities and doubts wailed at her that he was still faking it with her. He sure was good at it if he was, and Olli reassured herself with the memories of his kisses whenever she started to slide into the self-doubt.

"How long have you and Spur been together?" Charity asked.

"Just a couple of weeks," Olli said, her pulse jumping around inside her chest.

Charity nodded. "He's cute."

"Don't let him hear you say that," Olli said with a smile. "He's far too old to be *cute*." She picked up the empty sheet of labels and tossed it in the garbage can. "I'll get you an extra check for this week."

"Thanks, Olli." Charity grinned and picked up her purse. "I'm gonna go see if I can find me a cowboy as *cute* as Spur." She giggled, and Olli joined in. She had no idea where Charity would go to do that, but she wasn't twenty-two years old either.

"Be safe," she said to the girl as she left.

Olli then faced her perfumery, the enormity of the task in front of her threatening to crush her before she could begin. She pressed back against the exhaustion and the mess and told herself to start with just one thing.

The perfumery had four stations, two of which Olli worked at during the day as she created scents from the things she grew and-or combined those created scents together to make different perfumes or candles.

The third long row of stainless steel tables could really be divided in half. On the far end, she made perfumes; at the end closest to the door, she poured hand-melted wax for her candles. She made every candle and every bottle of perfume that left the shop.

The last station where she and Charity had been working was the packaging station, and it would be the easiest to clean up. She left it for Spur, and she moved to the scent table. Bins of flowers and fruits sat on the lower shelves, and Olli made sure they were all lidded properly. She picked up an empty plastic bin and started loading the remnants of her latest scent creation into it. Vials, tongs, leftover bits of wood, and paper towels. She made trip after trip to the garbage can, cleaning up the two stations where she spent most of her time.

She loved watching wax drip from a funnel too, but there was nothing like taking something she'd grown and distilling it down to its very essence. She inhaled deeply, trying to decide what her perfumery smelled like. These walls had experienced so many scents, and Olli liked to think just one particle of everything she'd ever done was trapped inside as a keepsake.

The door opened, and Spur walked in. Olli smiled at him, and he barely returned it. Nerves scattered through her body. "Hey," she said. "How was your day?"

"A day," he said, looking around. "Where do you want me?"

"I left the packaging station for you," she said. "It should be the easiest to organize. Anything that looks like trash, probably is. Boxes can be laid flat on the bottom shelves. I've got polish in here somewhere, and I'm going to start over here."

He nodded, and he seemed so tight tonight. She knew he

had a lot going on in his family right now, and she told herself his mood had nothing to do with her. He hadn't given her all the details about what was happening next door, but she knew enough to know he was stressed about it.

She pulled on a pair of black gloves to protect her hands from the polish and got to work. She hated the smell of the silver polish, because someone had thought it was a good idea to try to mask the metallic stink of it with oranges. All that did was produce two scents that had no business being together.

Olli scrubbed and wiped, growing sweaty with the workout it took to clean up months' worth of work. "I'm never going to let it get this bad again," she said, expecting Spur to respond.

He didn't, and Olli glanced over to the packaging station. He'd cleared it already, and he was wiping it down with an antibacterial wipe. She left the first station, which she'd just finished and joined him. "Wow," she said. "You're efficient."

He barely looked at her, and Olli felt like the ground beneath her feet might disappear. "Is everything okay?"

"Just fine," he said, moving away from her. He definitely wasn't fine. In the past, he'd never just come in and said nothing. He always kissed her hello, and he always had something to tell her from that day.

"You're the one who said it didn't matter what anyone thought of our relationship," she said. "As long as we were honest with each other."

"Yep."

"You're not being honest with me."

Spur froze, only his eyes lifting to hers. "You've got to be kidding me."

"You're not fine," she said, a tingle moving down her arms. "You're upset."

"Yeah, I'm upset." He straightened, his dark eyes blazing with black fire. "*You're* the one who hasn't been honest with *me*."

Olli frowned and cocked her head. "What are you talking about?" Her brain was so full of all the things she'd researched about Renlund United. She knew where the stores were, and how many there were. She knew how long Frank had been CEO, and she knew how they'd been founded out of a tiny town in Texas.

"I'm talking about how you told me that website where people put up dates they need? You know, for weddings and parties and stuff? You told me it was for creepers, that women shouldn't be on that site."

Olli said nothing, because she knew where this was going. "I only—"

"Guess who comes right up when you search in Dreasmville?" he said over her. "Olivia Blasted Hudson." He held up his phone. "Looking for a man with the perfect nose for a couple of hours." He read in a sarcastic voice. "Blaine told me. *Blaine*, Olli." He shook his head, his mouth pressed into a thin line.

"Why was Blaine on the site?" she asked, which totally wasn't the right question.

"He was investigating it for a friend," he said, his voice raw now. "By the way, he contacted you, and he'll be here next

Wednesday, as you asked him to be." Spur threw down the antibacterial wipe. "Maybe he can be your fake boyfriend for a couple of weeks." He glared at her as he strode by her. She turned, dumbfounded, and watched as he walked out of the perfumery without another word.

Olli flinched when the door swung closed, the slam loud and nearly deafening. "What just happened?" She looked at the half-clean perfumery, sure Spur would come back. When she'd overheard his half of a conversation with his mother, he'd chased after her.

Her mind racing as fast as her pulse, she peeled the gloves from her hands and tossed them onto the nearest table. Then she went after Spur.

Outside, the sun hung low in the sky, but Olli didn't need to look west. She faced east, wondering if Spur had driven or walked to her place. He'd done both in the past, and she hadn't heard his truck.

In the distance, she saw a horse galloping away from her, and she knew how he'd gotten there. "Spur!" she yelled, but he was way too far away to hear her. Desperation filled her, and she looked toward the house.

She went that way, because she needed car keys to get to Bluegrass Ranch, and they currently sat in a little basket on her kitchen counter. She retrieved them, her confidence and courage still strong. They stuck with her as she navigated the roads between her land and the ranch.

By the time she made it through the gates over there and had turned the wrong direction down not just one, but two, roads, Olli was fighting back tears. She pressed against them relentlessly, wishing she owned a horse and could just take the straightest path to Spur.

She finally pulled up to the house, where no less than four pickup trucks were parked. Her dinky sedan looked so out of place, and Olli also realized that she'd never been here before as Spur's girlfriend. She'd only stepped foot on the ranch the one time, for the picnic last weekend.

He always came to her house or they went out. She wasn't sure what to make of that, and she peered up at the impressive house. It was made of stone and siding, and someone took very, very good care of it. The landscaping was likewise pristine, and Olli struggled just to keep breathing.

There was no way she could get out of this car and go up to the door.

"Do it," she told herself. "You have to do it." Not only had Spur misunderstood, but Frank Renlund would be on her doorstep in less than twenty-four hours. She needed Spur, and she cursed herself for thinking she could use that website to get a few male testers for her new cologne.

Spur had already helped her, but she knew the basis for a good product was getting a lot of feedback before it was finalized. She'd been planning to mix up the top five colognes as identified by Spur, give the man she'd hired from the site twenty bucks and a sub sandwich for his time, and get the data she needed.

She'd done nothing wrong.

What did Spur think she'd done? He hadn't said before he'd left. She'd never seen him so angry, and her fingers shook as she reached for the door handle.

Get out, get up there, ring the doorbell, she recited mentally. She had to do this. It would be hard for less than sixty seconds.

She stood next to her car, the country stillness surrounding her so calm. The serenity of the scene reminded her of why she'd never left Dreamsville and why she'd decided to buy outside of town.

She couldn't move, because she just wanted to go home. She could change into her sweats and finish cleaning the perfumery in the morning.

No, you can't, she told herself. You have to do it tonight to get that polish smell out before Frank arrives. She started a mental argument with herself, and she honestly wasn't sure what to do.

"Olli?"

She blinked and turned toward the male voice. Trey stood there, and he glanced at the house and then her before detouring in her direction. "You okay? Do you need to see Spur?"

She nodded, because if Trey would take her to the door, she might be able to go.

"All right," he said with a smile. "C'mon then. We don't bite." He gestured for her to follow him, and he went past the trucks parked in the driveway and inside the garage. Olli hadn't even seen that it was open.

Trey went up the few steps there and opened the door, calling, "Is Spur around?" before he even stepped inside.

Olli lingered several paces behind him, but he didn't let the door close in her face. He held it for her as a couple of people answered his question.

"I'll see if I can find him," Trey said. "This place is kind of a zoo sometimes." He kept his smile in place and indicated she follow him again. He led her down a hall past a laundry room on one side and what looked to be a mud room with lots of storage, cowboy boots, jackets, hats, and other supplies on the other.

The hallway opened up into a massive kitchen and attached dining room. The ceiling stretched for two stories, and Olli's neck wouldn't bend back far enough to see everything. "Wow," she said.

"Looks like there's some dinner here," Trey said. "Help yourself. I'll be right back." He walked through the space and through a wide, arched doorway, where he began talking to a couple of the other Chappell brothers.

They all looked at her, and Olli had the distinct feeling she shouldn't be there. She certainly wasn't going to eat anything, though the meatballs and mashed potatoes didn't look half bad. Someone in this family could cook, and Olli snuck a glance at the men still talking on the other side of the room.

She just wanted to talk to Spur for a few minutes. She pulled out her phone and texted him. *Where are you? I just need five minutes to explain.*

He didn't answer, but Olli couldn't look away from her phone. She knew the moment she did, he'd respond.

Trey lifted his phone to his ear too, and he moved further into the house so she couldn't see him. He returned only a moment later and shook his head. At least she wasn't the only one he was ignoring.

Trey came back toward her. "No one knows where he is,"

he said. "I called him, but he didn't answer. Our best guess is he's in the stables. Did you want me to take you out there?"

Indecision raged through her. She did want to go out to the stables, and she didn't. "It's okay," she said. "I'm sure he'll call me back." She tried to put a smile on her face, but it didn't quite fit.

"...is what I'm saying," someone said behind her. It wasn't Spur, but Olli turned anyway. "You just can't—oh." Blaine stopped at the end of the hallway, a pretty blonde woman behind him.

"Have you seen Spur?" Trey asked.

Blaine held Olli's gaze for another moment and then looked at his brother. "Yes," he said slowly.

"Olli here needs 'im," Trey said. "Where is he?"

Blaine looked at the woman he'd come in with. Neither of them said anything.

"It's fine, guys," Spur said in the next moment, walking up behind the woman. It was as if he was Moses parting the Red Sea. All the people moved out his way, and he continued straight toward her. He did not look happy to see her, but he said, "Let's talk outside. You get five minutes."

CHAPTER 16

Spur led the way outside, wondering how Olli would categorize his walk. Probably as a stalk or a storm or a stomp. He'd seen her upset, and she'd taken a few minutes to calm down before she'd joined him on the steps the day she'd overheard him talking to his mother.

He took a deep breath, wishing he had a house full of air conditioning to have this conversation. He didn't want to have this talk at all, but he'd never been good at hiding how he felt, and when he'd gone to Olli's perfumery, he'd known she'd see right through him.

He exhaled and turned around after pacing away from the house to the shade of a big live oak. Olli walked toward him, her step less sure and less angry. She looked terrified of him, and some of Spur's anger deflated. He didn't want to be the Big, Bad Wolf. Not with Olli.

She stopped on the very edge of the shade and ran her

hands up and down her arms. She looked around. "Your place is really nice."

Spur blinked, because he didn't know what to say to that.

"You've never invited me over here," she said, looking at him.

Spur felt the weight of her displeasure, and he shifted his feet. "I didn't mean to be..." He waved his hand through the air. "Scary."

She tucked her hands into the pockets of her shorts. "You used to really intimidate me."

"Did I?"

"You're short and to the point," she said.

Spur nodded, because he was. "I forget sometimes that not everyone I'm dealing with is a horse or a dog."

"Or a sheep."

Spur ducked his head, his anger fading but his frustration lingering. "Why did you ask for men to meet with you on that website?"

"It's for testing," she said. "For my colognes. I have five I've fine-tuned based on your feedback, and I just wanted to narrow them to three. Then maybe to one." Her nervous energy hit him in the chest.

"Blaine said you didn't tell him any of that."

"It said for a couple of hours."

"Yeah, Olli. How long do you think it takes for a man to sleep with a woman?" He folded his arms, because how could she not get what she'd done? "How many men signed up?"

Olli's eyes blazed. "I don't have to answer to you, Spur." She turned away and started walking across the grass. "I can handle myself. I know what I have to do to make my products viable for the market, and that requires testing."

"Was my opinion not good enough for you?" he called after her, all of his fury returning. Why couldn't he ever be good enough for someone?

She didn't answer, and while Spur usually liked watching the woman walk away from him, he didn't right now.

He'd called after her before and chased after her previously. That was when he'd made a mistake. *She'd* made one this time, and while she'd come to talk to him, the few sentences she'd given him were not enough.

She'd made him spill his guts and confess his feelings for her. She'd never done that, and Spur had never needed her to. Until now.

He started after her, his long legs eating up the distance between them. "Olli," he called, and she spun back to him near her car.

"I don't know what else you want me to say," she said. "I am *trying* to expand my business, and I know how to do it. I got testers with my candles. Every scent I put out goes through a panel."

"I don't care about that," he said.

"What do you care about, Spur?"

"When I screwed up, I sat on your steps and told you exactly how I feel about you. You have never done that for me."

"This is about me having men over to do a panel on the colognes," she said. "I didn't tell anyone that we were just friends."

"How do you feel about me?" he asked.

Olli threw her hands up in the air. "Right now, I feel like I never want to see you again."

Spur started nodding. "Bad time to talk. All right. Go."

Olli's chest lifted and fell as she breathed heavily.

"I'll see you tomorrow," he said, his heart cracking because he didn't have the courage to end things with her. He'd started to fall for her last week while they danced the waltz, when she'd sang along with the country music at the concert, and when she brought him coffee while he replanted her lost flowers.

He'd fallen in love with her while she'd made cookies, burned her candles, and started studying to learn everything she could about Frank Renlund and Renlund United.

He fell in love with her a little bit more every time he looked into her eyes.

She cleared her throat. "I don't need you to come tomorrow."

Spur scoffed, because now she was just being ridiculous. "You said two o'clock, right?"

She shook her head. "I think it's stupid that I even need a boyfriend to get this grant, and I'm going to get it on my own." She nodded like that was that and pulled open her car's door.

"Are you breaking up with me?" he asked. "Or you just don't want me to come over tomorrow?"

"I'm going to tell Frank Renlund that I am a good businesswoman who provides amazing products for families—and I don't need a man to help me with it."

Spur just needed a yes or a no.

"I think it would be best if we did break-up," she said. "Then I won't be lying to him when I say I can—and have been—running my business boyfriend-free just fine, thank you very much."

Spur felt like he'd been struck dumb. No thoughts moved through his mind, and he didn't have anything to say to that.

"Thank you for your help with the colognes," she said. "I always appreciate my testers." She got in the car, settled her sunglasses on her face, and backed away from him.

He stood there and watched her car kick up dust as she went down the lane that led to the road. He watched her turn right and head back to her place. He watched the breeze blow through the trees in the front yard when he could no longer see Olli's car.

"Tester?" he asked, his brain finally catching up to what she'd said.

He wasn't exactly sure how long he stood there, but he managed to turn his head when Blaine said, "Spur?"

"Yeah?"

"It's starting to get dark. Come inside." Blaine touched his shoulder, and that got Spur to move. He followed his brother inside, and the TV blared too loud. It annoyed Spur, and he glared at his brothers in the living room. They all talked over the show, and he wished they'd been born with quieter voices.

He pulled a bowl from the cupboard and filled it with his favorite cereal.

"Spur," Blaine said.

"I'm fine," Spur said. He got the milk out and poured

plenty over the sugary puffs. "Really." He looked at Blaine, who wore concern in his eyes. "Go back to Tam. It's fine. I'm fine." He grabbed a spoon and took his dinner down the hall to his bedroom.

He had everything he needed here, and he wouldn't have to face anyone until morning. He ate his cereal and put on his horse rescue show. His fingers automatically moved to his knitting, and all he could think about was Olli as his hands moved through the stitches.

Nothing could sufficiently distract him tonight, though, and he set aside the yarn and needles and turned off the TV. He got to his feet and paced to the window. It didn't face west, and he couldn't see Olli's.

"What am I supposed to do?" he asked his faint reflection in the window. He knew she needed that grant. She'd been desperate enough to ask him to be her fake boyfriend almost two weeks ago to get it.

He didn't understand how him being concerned for her safety had brought them to a break-up. Sighing, he turned away from the window and collected his phone from the dresser.

When Tam leaves, can we talk? He sent the message to Blaine and got an answer in the affirmative almost instantly. One weight lifted, but Spur still felt like he wore a dozen ropes around his neck, all of them with a lead ball on the end of them, making him hunch over or fight to stand straight up.

Half an hour later, Blaine knocked on the door and came in. Spur looked over from where he lay on the bed, and he sat up. "Hey."

"Hey." Blaine closed the door behind him and moved over to the armchair in the corner. "What's going on?"

"I need some advice," Spur said, running his hands down his legs to his knees. He'd changed into a pair of gym shorts and a T-shirt, and if he could get his mind settled about tomorrow, he might be able to go to sleep.

"Okay," Blaine said. "About Olli?"

"Yes," Spur said. "It's not a terribly long story, but it starts with Olli asking me to be her fake boyfriend so she could get this grant she applied for."

"*Fake* boyfriend?" Blaine asked.

"It became real very soon after that," he said. "On the first date, actually." He looked down at his hands, his mind racing. "We talked about that. Admitted it." Mostly he'd admitted his feelings for Olli. "There was kissing, and I started helping her with this new men's line of colognes she's been working on. The investor is coming tomorrow, and I've promised her I'll be there."

"Then you have to be there," Blaine said.

Spur looked up and met his brother's eyes. "She told me tonight she doesn't need me. She thinks it's stupid to need a man to have a business and get a grant."

Blaine nodded, his head sort of rolling from side to side. "I can see her point."

"She broke up with me," Spur said. "She told me not to come."

"You want to go."

Spur started nodding, and he couldn't get himself to stop. "I want to go." Agony burned through him. "*Why* do I want to go? She wouldn't admit to me that she'd done anything wrong by using a *hook-up* website to get male testers for her cologne panel. She thinks she can do anything by herself—and she probably can. She's never confessed her feelings to me the way I have her, and then she just drove away from me like the last two weeks meant nothing to her."

He sucked in a breath and held it to force himself to calm down.

Blaine just watched him for a few seconds. "You want to go, because you want her to get the grant."

"Sure," Spur said.

"It's more than that."

Spur couldn't confirm or deny Blaine's statement, though it was absolutely more than that.

"You want to do what's right."

"Yes," Spur agreed. He'd always want to do what was right.

"You don't want to hurt her."

"No."

"But you don't want to be hurt either."

Spur swallowed and looked at the floor. "I've already been hurt."

"I can't tell you what to do," Blaine said. "I think you have to do the same thing here that you did with Katie."

Spur didn't want to walk away. He didn't want to go through that pain again, though his heart beat shallowly in his chest in much the same way it had when he'd signed the papers that made his divorce final.

"Follow your heart," Blaine said, standing. "Now, if you'll excuse me, I'm going to go do the same thing." He left, and it wasn't until the door clicked closed that Spur realized what he'd said.

"What?" he asked. As far as Spur knew, the only woman Blaine spoke to was Tam. Had he met someone else?

Thoughts of his brother only distracted him for a moment, and then he went right back to thinking about Olli and what he should do at two o'clock tomorrow afternoon.

CHAPTER 17

Blaine had been at war with himself for four days, and exhaustion threatened to overtake him. He knew he shouldn't make big decisions when in such a frame of mind, but he wanted to do what he'd just told Spur to do.

He wanted to follow his heart.

He kneaded the steering wheel, though it wasn't pliable, and kept driving. "You don't have to tell her everything," he said to himself. He didn't know what to tell her, though, and he should probably put together a speech before he showed up at Tam's. Otherwise, he might kiss her.

Blaine's mind blanked, and he made turns and arrived at Tam's without even realizing it. He sat in his truck, the giant engine rumbling when he didn't turn it off. He should just go, because he still didn't have any of the words to say to her.

He put his head down on the steering wheel and reminded himself that he was almost forty years old. He wasn't eighteen, and he wasn't even twenty-eight. Tam made him feel younger and like having a future together would be filled with joy and laughter.

"Blaine?"

He lifted his head at the muffled sound of Tam's voice through the glass. He looked at her, the single pane of glass separating them. He rolled it down, realizing he should've just gotten out of the truck.

She smiled at him. "What are you doing here? Did I forget something at the house?"

Blaine seized onto her question, as well as that bright smile that made his pulse pound a little harder. "Yes," he said, opening the door and getting out of the truck. He leveled his gaze at her and ignored the screaming nerves running through his whole body.

"You forgot me at the house," he said.

Tam's smile faltered, and a furrow appeared between her brows. "Blaine, you're not making any sense."

"You haven't put anything up on that website, have you?" Blaine knew she hadn't. He'd been checking it every day—possibly two or three times a day, which was how he'd found Olli's listing—to make sure he knew what Tam was doing.

"No," Tam said.

"What about the dating app?"

She shook her head, but again, Blaine knew she hadn't finished the registration on the app. He had, and he'd been waiting for her to pop into his feed.

Blaine wasn't sure how to convey his feelings for her. "I've been thinking—" he started at the same time Tam said, "Hayes called me, and—"

They both stopped talking, and Blaine's eyes widened. "He called you?"

"What have you been thinking about?"

Blaine retreated, not sure what to say now. He looked away, his mouth tightening.

"I didn't answer the call, Blaine," Tam said, stepping away. "You don't give me any credit." She cast him a dark look and headed back to her house.

Blaine got moving, and he hurried after her so that he darted up the steps to the porch before she reached the door. He put his palm flat against it and said, "Wait."

Tam sighed and looked up at him after a healthy pause. "What, Blaine?"

"I came because you forgot *me* at the house, Tam." He gazed down at her, feeling slightly drunk though he hadn't had a sip of alcohol in years and years. He didn't know what else to say, and it had been a while since he'd kissed a woman, but his hand slid up her arm easily. He tucked that luxurious blonde hair behind her ear, and he lowered his head until their mouths were only an inch apart.

"I'll be your boyfriend," he whispered, every sense on full alert. "If you want me to."

"Okay," Tam whispered, and Blaine went the rest of the distance and pressed his lips to hers. An explosion of heat moved through his mouth and down his throat, and Tam pulled in a breath and pushed her hands through his hair.

She kissed him like she'd thought about doing so before, and Blaine pulled away. "I've wanted to do that for a while."

"You have?" Tam giggled and moved her hands to his shoulders. Little fires broke out everywhere she touched.

"Yeah," Blaine whispered, opening his eyes.

Their eyes met, and Tam didn't giggle this time. "I've had a crush on you for what feels like forever."

Blaine blinked at her. "Why didn't you say anything?"

"You're my best friend, Blaine." She stepped out of his arms, some of the excitement of the past few moments dying. "I didn't—don't—want anything to be weird between us. I didn't—*don't*—want to lose you, and I figured if I said something and we dated and then broke up, I would've ruined everything between us."

Blaine's mind raced ahead again, and this time, he saw the future she mentioned. He didn't want to lose her either, and instant regret filled his head. "I shouldn't have kissed you," he said, backing up but meeting the door behind him. "I'm sorry. Sorry, Tam." He pushed his hands through his hair. "Oh, no, what have I done?"

He met her eyes briefly and stepped past her. "Sorry," he said over his shoulder. "I won't do it again." He flew down the steps, feeling like someone had strapped him to a wild roller coaster that went up, down, and around every few seconds.

"Blaine," she called after him, and he paused. He didn't turn around, but he didn't need to see her to hear her say, "Will you still be my boyfriend when Hayes comes into town?"

He twisted back to her, unable to fully commit to turning all the way around. "I never made the rules." He hadn't been able to do so, and he hadn't shown up for dinner at Mindie's either.

"I'll make them," she said from her spot at the top of the steps. "If you'll show up to dinner this time."

Blaine turned and considered her. "Did you show up last time?"

"Yes," she said, coming down the steps and stopping at the bottom. Several feet separated them, and blast it, all Blaine could think about was kissing her again. "I felt like a real idiot sitting there by myself, telling the waitress over and over that you were coming."

"I'm sorry," Blaine said, his apology count so high in the past few minutes he couldn't keep track of it. "I've been thinking about you, if that counts."

Tam cocked her head slightly, and they just looked at one another. "Is this what we're going to do? Pretend you didn't drive over here and admit you've wanted to kiss me for a while?"

"Yes," he said. "That's what I'd like you to do." He needed to turn this into something light, because what she'd said was absolutely true. He didn't want anything weird between them, and if a romantic relationship didn't work out between them, he'd lose her. They'd never be able to go back to what they were now.

"As for me, I'll forget you said you had a crush on me, and we'll make the rules and I'll be so good when Hayes comes into town. He'll really think we're so blissfully happy, and he'll see you're so over him, and then we can laugh about it after he leaves again."

Tam didn't smile or scoff, the way she sometimes did. When she stayed silent, he said, "Okay. Dinner tomorrow night? Is that enough time for the rules?"

She didn't move, and Blaine clapped his hands together. "Text me and let me know." He had to get out of there right now before he said or did something else that would embarrass himself further—or ruin every good thing he and Tam had.

He spun and strode away, got behind the wheel, and refused to look at Tam as he backed out of her driveway.

"You're such a loser," he muttered to himself.

His mother's words echoed through his head. *You had a perfectly good woman, Cayden, and you blew it.*

She'd been talking to Cayden about his latest girlfriend, but her statement could apply to Tam too. Had he really just blew everything with one kiss?

If he had, it had been a very, *very* good kiss, and Blaine found himself with a small smile on his face as he arrived back at Bluegrass Ranch.

He hurried back to Spur's room and knocked again.

"Yep," Spur said, and Blaine ducked inside.

"Okay, I just did something stupid and yet possibly amazing, and I need help."

Spur sat up, his eyes alight with interest. "Keep talking."

CHAPTER 18

"Yes," Tam said, her voice hushed though she lived alone, and Blaine had left twenty minutes ago. "He showed up here and *kissed* me."

"I just...I can't believe it," Cara said. "Was it a good kiss?"

Tam sighed and looked up at her ceiling. "Yes," she said. "Amazing. Not long enough, though, and then I ruined it all." She proceeded to tell her sister the rest of the story, ending with, "That's it. He drove away."

"But you're going to dinner with him tomorrow."

"I don't know," Tam said. "He didn't show up last time, and I'm planning to be at least half an hour late, just to be sure. I might actually text Trey and find out if Blaine has left for the restaurant before I even get in the shower." Her chest pinched as a replay from earlier in the week moved through her mind. It had been on a loop for days, and Tam had barely slept the past few nights.

"Do you need help with the rules?" Cara said.

"I know Blaine," Tam said. "The rules will take ten seconds." He'd have put *no kissing* on it, but they'd already broken that rule.

He won't again, Tam thought. Blaine had an iron will, and he stuck to things he'd decided to do like glue. The man lifted weights six days a week, no matter what. He'd barely left the ranch after his break-up with Alex, and Tam knew he'd decided to simply surround himself with family and never date again.

"You know what they say," Cara said. "Rules are made to be broken. Put everything on the list that you really want to do, Tam. Then shatter those things." She laughed, and Tam let the infectious nature of it put a smile on her face too.

"Okay," she said. "Enough about me. What about you and Chris?"

"Oh, Chris," Cara said. "He's being an idiot, because he thinks we're too young to get married."

Cara was a decade younger than Tam, but, "Twenty-five is not too young to get married," Tam said.

"I know," Cara said. "He is a year younger than me, and he wants to finish law school first."

"Have a long engagement then," Tam said.

"I'm going to let it be for right now," Cara said. "He sometimes gets too far inside his head."

"Right," Tam said, and she realized that she could've said the exact same thing about Blaine. He was incredibly smart, and he got lost inside his mind sometimes too. "All right, I'll let you go."

She hung up with her sister and stayed on the bed for another minute. Then she quickly tapped out a text to Blaine.

Dinner tomorrow night. I'll come pick you up at 6:30.

He didn't answer right away, not that she expected him to. Blaine would shut down for a while after an encounter like the one they'd just had. She'd shut down while he was still talking on the sidewalk.

Her mind was moving again now, though. She'd heard the tell-tale rumble of his engine when he'd pulled into her driveway, and she'd given him a minute to come inside. When he hadn't, and he'd leaned over the steering wheel, she'd gone out to him. She'd thought maybe he'd fainted or didn't feel well and had just pulled over at her house, because he knew it.

You forgot me at the house.

Blaine didn't understand that he was impossible to forget.

Rule #1: The relationship will not ruin our friendship.

Sent.

Rule #2: The relationship will only be binding while Hayes is in town.

Sent.

Rule #3: No kissing.

Sent.

Rule #4: Public displays of affection will be limited to flirting, laughing, and hand-holding and only for the purpose of perpetuating the relationship's validity for others.

Sent.

Rule #5:

Sent.

I don't really have a fifth rule, she sent. *If you do, feel free to add it.*

She saw the *delivered* status next to the texts change to *read* in a blink of an eye, and her heartbeat shot to the top of her head.

He started typing, and Tam smiled though she wished she wouldn't. "You can't romanticize everything he does," she told herself.

Dinner at 6:30 is great.

I don't need any rules, Tam, he said next, and she sat up in bed, reading the text over and over.

Especially not #3.

Her mouth turned dry, and she blinked, her vision turning white. When she could see again, the text was still there.

She fumbled her phone trying to get it to make a call, and she ended up bobbling it, then hitting it with her knuckles as she tried to grab it. It flew away from her, hit the wall, and then landed with a terrible cracking sound against the floor.

"No," she said, disturbing her dogs as she went after it. She picked up the phone and found the screen splintering right before her eyes. She tried to tap, and nothing happened.

"Great." She knelt on the floor, her ruined phone in her hands, and looked up at the ceiling. "Is this a sign or something? Why can't I be with Blaine Chappell?"

In her mind, the two of them were so good together, and she'd be happy for the rest of her life with him at her side.

Tam stared at her phone, the screen bright but obviously not doing anything. It was too late to go to the cell phone store tonight.

"Tomorrow," Tam said, because she wasn't one to just roll over and give up. She couldn't respond to Blaine, and she drove herself toward being completely crazy as she imagined the fun, flirty texts she and Blaine could've exchanged all night.

Her fantasies ran wild until she finally drifted into unconsciousness.

CHAPTER 19

Olli organized, cleaned, scrubbed, and polished, her tears dormant. She let her anger drive her to get the perfumery spic and span. When it was spotless, she stood back, her gloves hanging from a couple of fingers.

In the morning, she'd return and put out the fresh flowers she'd cut from her garden. The three new scents she'd developed for next quarter sat on the end of the table nearest to the entrance, and she was ready to show them all to Frank Renlund.

She had note cards she'd go over in the morning one last time, and she had a new speech she needed to prepare. Surely Frank would ask her about her boyfriend or husband, and she needed to be assertive without being defensive.

She nodded to the perfumery, as it was all she had left. Turning away from the sterile room, she left the building and headed home. After tossing the gloves in the trashcan, Olli washed up in the kitchen sink, scrubbing all the way to her elbows.

She looked out the window above the sink, the lights at the ranch twinkling. A sob gathered in her stomach and grew. When it was too big to hold back, it surged up her throat and out of her mouth. She spun away from the lights and sank to the floor, everything she felt for Spur flowing through her.

He'd sat right on her steps and admitted how he felt about her. She'd never told him in so many words, but she'd thought her actions had shown him how she felt. She could hear his voice in her head, so demanding and so desperate to know how she felt about him.

"Of course your opinion is important," she said amidst her tears. "It's the only one I care about." She could make him a personal cologne, but if she wanted to sell the masses of male cologne wearers, it was smart business to do a test panel. "Why didn't he understand that?"

The better question was why Olli hadn't just walked away without breaking up with him. "You always take things one step too far," she told herself, her self-loathing combining with the fact that she'd failed again.

She cried right there in the kitchen, wishing her cat wasn't a hermit or that she had a dog to come lick her salty tears from her face. When her tailbone ached and her legs had started to go numb, she got to her feet and headed down the hall to her bedroom.

She lit her Serenity candle and placed it on her nightstand. She changed into her pajamas and used the body spray she hadn't released to the public yet. It was called Sleep, and she'd infused it with lavender, jasmine, and warm vanilla.

Most people didn't know there was a difference between warm vanilla and cold vanilla, but Olli knew. Other things produced a rounder, more whole scent when warmed, and she always toasted almonds and cinnamon before infusing them into oils.

Almonds were not very pleasing, and Olli had given up using nuts of any kind in her concoctions.

She picked up the tester bottle of cologne she'd made for her demo tomorrow and spritzed her pillow with it. While that dried, she went through her nightly routine, hating looking into her bloodshot eyes and seeing her wet eyelashes. When her skin was clean and her teeth brushed, she exhaled heavily as she climbed into bed.

She took an extra pillow from the other side of the bed and hugged it as she rolled onto her side, her misery complete and endless. The notes of Spur's cologne—literally a cologne she'd created and named after him—floated into her nose and reminded her so much of the man she'd started to fall in love with.

She wasn't sure how she fell asleep, but the next thing she knew, her alarm woke her.

"It's Saturday," a woman's voice chirped. "Time to get up and make this weekend the best one yet."

She reached over and swiped off the alarm, which was a thirty-second snippet of a wellness podcast that repeated if she didn't turn it off in time. She always turned it off on time, as she wasn't a very heavy sleeper.

She went through the motions of getting ready for the day. Ginny had laid out her clothes days ago, and she stepped into the navy blue pencil skirt and bright purple blouse. The silk flowed around her arms and hid her extra weight. She'd cover it with a white jacket that would give her polish and class, but she didn't need to wear that until the last minute.

She stepped into a tasteful pair of navy heels and clicked her way into the kitchen to make coffee. She draped her jacket over the back of a dining room chair and went over her notecards while her coffee brewed. She sipped half a cup before her stomach told her to stop as it was boiling enough already.

Armed with the vase of flowers she'd arranged yesterday, her notes, and her jacket, she went to the perfumery. She made sure everything was sitting just-so, and she stood back and snapped a couple of pictures of the room to send to Ginny.

Her carefully constructed happiness stared back at her on her screen, and she wanted to scream and start throwing the nearest objects she could get her hands on.

That's beautiful! Ginny sent back. *Good luck today. I can't wait to hear all about it.*

Olli couldn't wait to tell her about it. She looked up after confirming that she'd call as soon as she could, and she found herself wishing she didn't have to handle or entertain Frank Renlund alone. If she'd known that from the beginning, she'd be ready, but she'd been counting on Spur being at her side.

"It's your fault," she whispered, and the clean perfumery seemed to capture the words and echo them back to her.

She couldn't stand the thought of him being hurt and upset, and she knew he'd be both. Spur was a big man, but that only meant he felt big things too. He possessed a big heart to go with those hands she loved so much, and she spun and went outside, the air inside the perfumery suddenly too heavy and too full of the wrong scents.

She pulled in breath after breath until she calmed down. She brushed her hair off her forehead, hoping she hadn't ruined the gentle wave she'd put in it that morning. She hadn't cried, so she knew her makeup was still flawless.

An alarm sounded on her phone, and she straightened her spine and her shoulders. "You can do this," she said. "You opened this perfumery with eight scents and three hundred dollars in the bank."

In the past seven years, sometimes her bank account had been lower than that. Olli had dug in and worked harder. She ran sales on her perfumes to get more product out into the world. She learned online ads and started profiting more and more.

She'd fixed up the old equipment shed on her property, turning it into the perfumery over the course of a year as she continued to work out of her kitchen and save money for the renovations. She'd never looked back.

If she didn't get this grant money, she would not be beaten. She would find another way to develop her men's line and get it out into the world.

"You can do this," she said again, silencing the alarm, which had signaled she had ten minutes before Frank Renlund and his assistant, Benjamin, would arrive.

She went back into the perfumery and tossed her note-cards into the garbage. She put her top five samples of colognes on the far table, where she distilled scents into oils. She was ready.

Good thing, too, because she'd only taken one more breath before the sound of tires crunching over gravel met her ears. She quickly put on her jacket and made sure every layer of fabric lay in precisely the right spot.

Then she went outside, painting a perfect smile on her face. Spur had said that her smile could light up the whole state, and she'd never gotten such a great compliment from a man before.

A man wearing a dark suit had already emerged from the driver's seat of the car, and he stood at the back door of a shiny, black Towncar. They exchanged a glance, and Olli assumed him to be Benjamin.

He opened the door, and another man straightened. He also wore a suit that couldn't get any blacker. Frank Renlund stood taller than Benjamin, and while he had a pair of broad shoulders, he was very thin.

He buttoned his jacket and smiled at Benjamin, who came toward her first.

"You must be Olivia," the man said, and Olli recognized his voice from the phone calls she'd had with him.

"Yes," Olli said, just as smoothly. "You can call me Olli." She shook Benjamin's hand. "I'm glad you're here, Benjamin." She turned her attention to Frank. "Welcome to Fluency, Mister Renlund."

"Happy to be here," Mr. Renlund said. "You can call me Frank."

"All right." Olli looked between the two men. "Should we go in?"

"Yes, please," Frank said.

Olli turned, but Benjamin slipped between her and the door and opened it. She smiled at him. "Thank you." She entered the perfumery, the jittery feeling in her chest subsiding now that the introductions were over. "Here we are." She stepped out of the way to make room for the others and surveyed the space.

"I develop all my scents here," she said, her voice falling easily into that tone she'd used as a tour guide. That was all this was. A tour of Fluency.

"At that far table there." She indicated the far table on the right. "Each quarter, I develop three new scents for my candle subscription box members. They get the brand-new, exclusive scent every month, and that scented candle is available for that month only. The bestsellers make a reappearance at some point in the future, so I never waste stock, and I get an idea of what my customers like."

She stepped over to the table where she'd set her future scents. "After I make the scents, I create the products at the second station. I've been making perfume for over a decade, and candles for five years. I'm expanding to men's scents in the very near future." She picked up the first candle, which she'd named Return to Childhood.

Olli faced the two men and held out the teal, peach, and pink swirled candle. "You can take a sniff and let me know what you think."

Frank held her eye for an extra moment, a small, knowing

smile on his face, before he bent to smell the candle. "Mm," he said. "Smells like my cold cereal as a boy."

Olli grinned at him. "Did you actually eat cold cereal, Mister Renlund?" She turned to Benjamin. He took a sniff of it, the hard look he wore on his face never slipping.

"It smells like sugar," he said.

"Warm sugar," Olli corrected. "My signature tutti fruity scent is a big winner with my customers, and that's the top note in this candle. Sugar is the middle layer, and I did a milk honey base to bring back that nostalgia of cold cereal."

She turned the label toward Mr. Renlund. "I name each scent for what it represents." This one, she'd put Saturday Morning Cartoons, Dessert for Dinner, and Wasting Time.

He grinned wider. "It's great," he said, glancing around. "I know what you do, Olli. All of this was in your application, and since it was well-organized and documented, you caught my eye."

"These things got you to the top," Benjamin said. "We really just like to come meet the applicants."

Olli looked from Mr. Renlund to Benjamin, seeing her presentation slip away from her. "All right," she said, swallowing. "What would you like to know?" She glanced at her cologne samples and back to Benjamin. His smile had disappeared while Frank's had stayed hitched in place.

"I thought your boyfriend was going to be here," Benjamin said, his eyes a cool blue that matched his voice.

Olli's first inclination was to lie. Tell them that something had come up for Spur. He'd told her that animals were unpredictable, and there could be any number of excuses that would keep him from being there with her.

She pushed against that, because she did want to be honest in her business, and she believed in her ability to run this company the way she always had.

"I don't have a boyfriend," she said, her voice strong but about to crack. She swallowed and breathed in deeply. "I built this business with eight scents, building different combinations in my kitchen. I designed the labels for the first three years, and I printed them at my local copy store. Every month was a struggle, but the business grew."

She switched her gaze to Frank, as Benjamin's eyes were starting to give Olli a chill. "I expanded to candles. My bottom line grew and grew. I learned advertising and the power of social media. I know you have four hundred and four stores across the country, and I know where my new line of men's colognes will sell the best."

She took a breath, almost to the end of her speech. "I didn't do any of that with a boyfriend. Well." She shrugged, her head bobbing from side to side for a moment. "I've had men come and go in my life, some during this and some before. Some supported me, and some didn't."

She shook her head, determined not to let her emotions into this. "The point is, Mister Renlund, that I don't need a boyfriend or a husband to run this business." She met Benjamin's eye and felt the fire burning in her soul. "You told me to get one, even for a few days. I didn't want to get this grant because of that. There are eight men who live next door, and I could've asked any of them to play a part for me. I want to *earn* this grant, because my products are superior, and because they'll fit right into the Renlund United brand."

"You think perfumes and scented candles are unique?" Benjamin asked.

"Mine are," Olli said. "Renlund United serves a large general population, seventy-eight percent of which is female. I know women, gentleman. Even if we already have a bottle of perfume we love, we're looking for the next one. We want a candle in every room. Sometimes more than one, because we never know what our mood is going to be when we get home from work, or how we'll feel after making dinner, or how exhausted we'll be once the children finally go to bed."

"If only twenty-two percent of our customers are male, why do we need men's scents?" Mr. Renlund asked.

"Every man wants to smell his best for the woman he's hoping to impress," Olli said, echoing something Spur had told her. He was there with her, and Olli smiled as if she were about to kiss him. "Every woman wants her man to smell amazing when he shows up to take her out for a night of dinner and dancing. She wants to go home with his crisp, blue, peppery, or clovey scent on her clothing. Then she can smell him again and again, fantasizing about when he'll finally kiss her, or when he'll call, or if she should text him to say what a great time she had."

Her throat closed, and she had to stop talking. She took advantage of the moment to look back and forth between the two of them, both of them watching her with keen, intelligent eyes. "My scents are uniquely cowboy," she said. "Women across the country adore cowboys, because they represent what we all love: country, animals, and God."

Benjamin's eyebrows went up, but he didn't say anything.

"Let me get this straight," Frank said. "You're selling men's cologne...to women."

Olli grinned at him. "Precisely, Mister Renlund," she said. "Any businesswoman who's smart knows that every product should be developed with the purchasing woman in mind. *We're* the ones who buy the majority of the items in our homes, from children's toys, to household products, to everything for our men."

Frank and Benjamin exchanged a glance, and Olli took a deep breath. "Now, if you don't want to go through the other candles, which I will point out are fabulous *and* exclusive, I have some prepared scents for the men's line to show you."

Before either of them could accept or decline her invitation, the door to the perfumery opened. Spur walked in, and Olli let out a gasp.

"Hey, sweetheart," he said easily, his face handsome and worry-free. "Sorry, I'm late. Animals can be unpredictable." He moved to her side, and she saw the flawless jeans, the boots that had never touched ranch dust, and the cowboy hat he wore to church. He bent down and kissed her, and Olli gave a nervous, mostly breathless laugh.

She looked at Benjamin and Frank, and they now both had their eyebrows up, their eyes wide, and plenty of curiosity radiating from them.

CHAPTER 20

S pur's heartbeat crashed against his ribs, but he kept his smile in place. The two men facing him and Olli looked like they'd stepped off the pages of a fashion magazine, and Spur had the distinct feeling that he'd walked into a nest of snakes.

Olli had let him kiss her, so that was one reason for his accelerated pulse. He knew it wasn't the only reason though.

"What did I miss?" he asked, glancing at Olli and back to the two men. He had no idea which one was the CEO and which one the assistant.

"You missed the part where Olivia said she didn't have a boyfriend."

Spur sucked in a breath and turned to Olli. "You told them?"

"We broke up," she hissed, her eyes flashing without the fire. Had she forgiven him? Did she regret her decision?

"It was just a discussion," Spur said, not caring about the

other two men in the room. "I was concerned for your safety, Olli. You're the one who said that site was dangerous, and I wanted to make sure you were okay."

"I know that." Olli looked down, a sigh escaping her mouth. Her hands fiddled with his tie, and Spur sure did like that, "I made sure everyone knew it was for a testers panel this morning."

"Good move," Spur said. He flicked a look at one of the men. "I know you don't need a boyfriend to get this grant, but I also know that I still want to be that boyfriend. I've told you before, Olli, but I don't want to be your friend or your neighbor. I want to be your boyfriend. Heck, I want more than that. I want to spend my life with you."

"Spur," she said, her eyes widening as she looked up into his.

"You don't have to tell me how you feel right now," he said quickly. He leaned forward, a small smile playing with his mouth. "I would like to hear it eventually, though. A man starts to wonder how a woman feels about him if it's not said." He kept his voice soft and his mouth right against Olli's ear.

Her hand slid up his chest to his neck, and Spur shivered. "I love you, Olli. Please don't push me away over this." He straightened and looked at her, his eyes searching hers. She nodded, tears gathering in her eyes.

She faced the two men as well, and said, "Gentlemen, this is Spur Chappell. He owns the ranch next door, and we've been seeing each other." She indicated the man on her right. "This is Benjamin Radcliff."

"Nice to meet you, sir," Spur said, stepping slightly away from Olli to shake the man's hand.

"And Frank Renlund."

Spur shook his hand too, cataloguing the look the two men exchanged. They looked almost identical, though Benjamin's hair was a shade lighter than Frank's. He also carried more weight and looked healthier overall. They could be a decade older than Spur or only five years. He wasn't sure. What he was sure about was his decision to get dressed up and get over to the perfumery.

"Can we just take a break?" Olli asked. "I need five minutes alone with Spur." She stepped through the men and opened the perfumery door. "If you could just wait out here."

"They don't need—" Spur started, cutting off when Frank said, "Take your time," and walked out. Benjamin followed him, and Olli laughed lightly.

"Thank you, gentlemen. It really will just be a minute." She closed the door and faced it, her shoulders rising as she took a long breath in.

"I'm sorry," Spur said before she turned around. Maybe he'd misread her signals, but his neck still tingled from where she'd touched it. "I didn't know you'd already told them you didn't have a boyfriend."

She faced him then, her emotions flying across her face. "You love me?"

"Desperately," he said. "I know it's only been two weeks, and that it's fast." Boy, did he know that. "I know that. I just don't want to deny how I feel about you. If you're not ready for that, I get it. We can date as long as you want. I just don't want you to break up with me because of a principle. Because you're trying to prove to those guys that you don't need me to run Fluency. We already know that, and if they don't know it, that's their problem."

He took a breath, because he thought he'd said quite enough. Spur had done what he could do, and she held the ball now. What she did with it was her choice, and he'd figure out a way to live if she dropped the ball and shattered his heart.

He really hoped she wouldn't do that, though.

"I do need you, Spur," she said, her voice pitching up. "I need you desperately." A tear splashed her cheek, and she quickly wiped it away. "I may not be all the way in love with you yet, but I think it'll take just one more night at Six Stars, and you'll have my heart completely."

Spur couldn't believe what he was hearing. "One more night, huh?"

A laugh exploded out of her mouth, and Spur wanted to wrap her up tightly in his arms and keep her there for a long time. "You've won my heart already, Olli. I think I fell for you the moment I smelled that perfume, before we even went to Six Stars for the first time."

"Even though you take all your first dates there?" She took a playful step toward him, her head down.

"A man likes to have a plan," he said. "In a comfortable place."

"Next time we go, will you wear your signature scent?"

Spur's eyes widened. "I have a signature scent?"

She lifted her gaze to him. "Yep. It's called Spur, and it's got Strength, Security, and Sexy Cowboy in it. Women everywhere will be buying it for their boyfriends, and every man across the country will smell like you." She touched the end of his tie and slid her fingers up his chest.

"Do you have some I can smell?" he asked, his voice catching on itself.

"I sure do," she said. "I'll show you after you give me a proper make-up kiss."

"I can do that," Spur said, loving the way she didn't just use her nose to smell, and he took the woman into his arms and kissed her. It was just as hot as the first time they'd kissed, but Spur forced himself to pull away sooner. She had two big businessmen waiting for her outside.

"I'd love to smell that," one of them said, and Olli spun toward the door. No one had come through it, though the voice had sounded like it was in the same room with them. She emitted a little shriek as she moved away from him and to the window. She yanked the cord to lift the blinds, and Spur saw the window. It was wide open.

Benjamin stood there, a smile on his face. "I really want to smell that, and if it's something women everywhere will buy for their boyfriends, I want it in all our stores."

Olli just stood there, so Spur walked to the door and opened it. Frank and Benjamin re-entered the perfumery, and Benjamin actually stepped forward. "I'm not Benjamin Radcliffe," he said. "My real last name is Renlund, and my brother and I run this company together."

"You're kidding," Olli said, looking from him to Frank.

"I like you, Olli," Benjamin said. "You didn't ignore me like I was the hired help. You spoke to me as if I were as important as Frank." He looked at his brother, who was nodding and smiling. "First one in this round."

"She's our last," Frank said. "That makes her the *only* one."

"Right," Benjamin said. "I like that, Olli. I like this perfumery you have here. I like all the things you two just said to one another." He glanced down the tables, and Spur followed his gaze. "I've been married for twenty-two years, and I can admit that my marriage has lost some of its...spice. If I go home with that cologne, and it does half of what you're promising, I really will put it in all four hundred and four of our stores."

Olli flew into action then, and Spur could lose hours watching her in her element. "Your wife is going to *love* this," she said, returning to the group with a small bottle of clear liquid. "I'd make it amber, like the color of a beautiful saddle." She glanced at Spur. "But I don't do colorings on samples. Now, does your wife like a more peppery, crisp scent, or the warmer cloves and cedars? Because I have one called City Slicker too, that is going to be every bit as fabulous as Spur." She glanced at him, a shy smile touching her mouth. "Well, maybe second best to Spur, but still wonderful. It'll hit the opposite end of the spectrum from Spur, which is where we find the majority of colognes for men."

"I honestly don't know," Benjamin said. "She's always buying me Radiant Water for my birthday."

"Okay," Olli said. "That's the crisper, blue scents. You want Spur." She lifted the bottle, a beautiful smile on her face. "My boyfriend trains champion horses that run in the

Kentucky Derby—some of them win too. So the base note here is actually genuine leather. It provides a warm base without much acid. Above that is a scent I use often in my candles, but not so much in my perfumes. Cotton. Spur is always dressed to the nines when he comes to pick me up. His clothes are clean, he's wearing boots that have *never* seen a horse, and his hat is one a proper cowboy would wear to church on Sunday."

Spur reached up and touched that hat, grinning at Olli.

"That middle scent gives you the crisp, clean scent we associate with men's fragrances. The top note is blue. For Spur, it represents the sky and the clouds. It's not as cold as ice or water—as what your wife buys for you—but it's still got that freshness and lightness you're looking for in a partner. It's not going to knock your date over the head with the smell, but it's going to linger with her after you drop her off."

Olli sprayed the cologne into the air. "One misconception is that a person should spray their cologne right onto their skin. It's actually better for it to be on your clothes. Women should get it in their hair."

"You should do videos to go with your products," Spur said, and Olli beamed at him.

"Great idea." She turned back to Frank and Benjamin. "Sort of a how-to-wear-a-scent-and-get-your-man."

"Or woman," Benjamin said.

"Or woman," Olli agreed. "Spur, can you be our model?"

"Absolutely." He stepped to Olli's side, a new hope blooming inside him that he'd always be right here at her side, helping her with what she needed the way she helped him with what he needed.

Olli did her demo, and she spritzed and sprayed all three of them before she finished. They took Frank and Benjamin next door to the ranch, and Spur showed them the horses he'd been working with.

"We're hopin' to sell her for seven-fifty," he said, gazing at Lucky Number Thirteen, who he'd just introduced to everyone.

"Thousand?" Benjamin asked.

"That's right." Spur smiled at Lucky, who really just wanted a treat.

"We're in the wrong business," Frank commented, and Spur chuckled. His hand in Olli's felt just right, and the afternoon had been one of his best.

"Your shoes would never last a day on a ranch," Olli said, and the four of them laughed. "Who's ready to go to dinner? I picked out the perfect place for someone who's never been to Kentucky."

Later that night, after all the handshakes and goodbyes, Spur loosened his tie and sat down on Olli's couch. She'd kicked off those sexy heels and gone into the kitchen to get them something to drink. She joined him on the couch, offering him a bottled iced tea. She tucked her legs under her and faced him, sitting sideways on the couch.

He looked at her, and she looked at him, and everything

that was a little cracked between them mended. "How do you feel?" he asked.

"Good," she said, her voice a touch high. "They said I'd know by midweek."

Spur nodded, because he'd been standing right there when Frank had said it. He twisted the cap on his tea, satisfied with the resulting *pop!* as the lid released.

"How do you feel?" Olli asked, supporting her head with one hand while the fingers on her other went up his forearm.

"Like the luckiest man in the world," he said.

She smiled at him. "Why's that?"

"Because I got to spend the afternoon with the sexiest, smartest woman I've ever met. She forgave me for acting irrationally, and I'm sitting on her couch, hoping to kiss her." He grinned at her and took a drink of his tea.

"You always give better answers than me," she said, and she sounded mildly annoyed by it too.

"You can fix that," he said.

"How?"

"Tell me how you feel." He looked at her and refused to let her look somewhere else.

"Like the luckiest woman in the world."

"Why's that?"

"Because there's this really great man, who smells amazing, and always looks amazing, and he's got these amazing hands."

Spur chuckled and shook his head. "Enough with the *amazing*."

"I pushed him away, but he wouldn't go. He came back,

and he apologized when *I* was the one who acted irrationally and took things just a little too far."

Spur looked at his iced tea bottle then.

"He loves me, and he wants what's best for me. He's strong, and smart, and literally the best kisser on the planet."

"Wow, he really does sound amazing," Spur said quietly.

Olli exhaled and snuggled into Spur's side. "I realized I don't need another date at Six Stars to fall in love with him. I'm already there."

Spur smiled and closed his eyes, hanging onto those words and committing them to memory.

"I'm sorry, Spur. Thank you for coming today."

He leaned forward and put his bottle on the coffee table in front of them. Then he took hers and set it next to his. Their eyes met, and Spur reached out with one of his amazing hands, wondering what she liked about it so much. He cradled her face in his palm, enjoying the way she leaned into his touch.

"I love you, Olli."

"I love you too, Spur."

He kissed her, and kissing Olli really was a life-changing experience that Spur couldn't define with words. He didn't need to hear more; he could feel how Olli felt about him in every stroke of her mouth against his.

CHAPTER 21

Tam's heartbeat pulsed super fast in her chest as she made the turn onto Bluegrass Ranch. She wished it wouldn't, but she couldn't seem to control her heartbeat. It did what it wanted, no matter what directions she gave it.

She breathed in slowly, because that sometimes worked to help her calm down, but no amount of deep breathing was going to settle her.

She was picking up Blaine Chappell for dinner, and that was simply outrageous. Part of her hoped he'd be sitting on the front steps, waiting for her. All of her hoped that, actually, because she didn't want to go up to the front door and ring the doorbell. If he wasn't outside, she'd just go in the garage entrance, because Tam couldn't remember the last time she'd used the Chappell's front door.

If his driveway wasn't so dang long, Tam would know what she had to do already.

Her phone blitzed out a bubbling sound, and she looked at the radio screen in her truck. *Just text me when you get here. I'll...*

From Blaine.

"Even better," Tam muttered. She could text him that she was waiting outside, like he'd done for her when he'd picked her up for high school for the few months they'd carpooled. The real problem was she didn't want the same relationship with Blaine now that she'd had then. She didn't want a ride-share friend she texted when she got to his house.

She'd never actually done that, because she hadn't had a phone back then. Only the rich had beepers and the earliest cell phones, which meant that Blaine had definitely had one. Bluegrass Ranch screamed of the wealth the Chappell's had, and Tam had never asked Blaine how much would be his. He'd never volunteered the information either, and Tam found herself wondering.

There were eight brothers. How much would they each get? How much of the ranch did they own? Or did one of them own it, and the others got paid a salary?

Tam arrived at the house, still no closer to a solution for her new relationship with Blaine. She didn't want to text him, so she parked and got out of her truck. She glanced around the front yard and headed for the garage, her step sure.

She'd showered in the mid-afternoon, and she'd put on a clean pair of jeans. She saw no point in opting for a skirt or a dress, as she literally only wore such things to church. She didn't want Blaine to think she was trying too hard. She didn't want Blaine to think she wanted him to kiss her again, though she did.

She'd put on a pale pink blouse with big, splashy sailboats all over it, and she'd paired her clothes with her cowgirl boots. She'd curled her blonde hair, but that was nothing new. The makeup she wore was a little new, because Tam saw no point in brushing foundation and blush on her face only to sweat it off as she wrestled with leather.

She sometimes wore makeup to church, but she sometimes woke too late and rushed out the door with her earrings in her hand. She'd put them in on the drive to the chapel, and she'd sit on the side with her mom, who always had a warm smile for her—and the question about who she was seeing.

Tam hadn't been to church in a while, to say the least.

She went into the garage and up the steps to the door that led into the house. The Chappells had a mudroom that was more like personalized storage for the men that lived there, along with a laundry room right off the entrance. Sometimes they came in from the ranch mighty dirty, and Blaine's father had been smart with the design of the homestead.

Down the hall sat the kitchen, and Tam went that way, hearing a few men's voices echo back to her.

"...that's all I'm saying," Duke said.

"I know what you're saying," Trey said. "But I don't believe it." He turned to put something back into the fridge, and his eyes caught on Tam's. "Oh, hey, Tam."

"Hey, Trey." She smiled and coached herself not to reach up and tuck her hair behind her ear.

"Blaine's on the back deck. Our mother called."

Tam looked right, where the back deck was. "Could be hours."

"Nah, he has a date tonight," Trey said with a grin. "He said he can't be late."

"A date?" Tam's pulse raced again, and she glanced at Trey. "Blaine?"

"Right?" Trey laughed and picked up his bowl of cereal. "He wouldn't say who it was with, but when Ma called, he rolled his eyes and said, 'I don't have time for this.'"

"He still answered."

"Yes, he did. Blaine is *such* a momma's boy."

Tam knew that, and she actually found it charming and endearing. He cared about his mother, and out of all the boys, he was the one who stuck up for her the most.

"You look nice," Duke said, scanning Tam as he went past her. "Blaine's all dressed up too." He continued down the hall, calling, "I'm headed out with Alli. Don't wait up for me."

"You don't even live here," Trey called after him, but Duke just went out the door without another word.

"I'll call Blaine tomorrow," Tam said, not daring to meet Trey's eye. "Don't want to interrupt his date." She turned and walked down the hall too, somewhat annoyed that she couldn't just say she was Blaine's date.

"Hey, Tam, wait a second," Trey called after her.

She considered continuing as if she hadn't heard him. That seemed like it would be impossible, so she paused with her hand on the doorknob and barely twisted back to the kitchen. "Yeah?"

The sound of his boots against the tile floor met her ears, and he switched on the light in the hall. His eyes slid down her body to her feet and back. "You do look nice tonight."

"Thanks," she said. "I'm—"

"Are you going out with Blaine?" Trey interrupted.

Tam opened her mouth to respond, but words seemed to fail her.

"Someone has to go check Mom's dishwasher." Blaine's loud voice carried all the way to where Tam and Trey stood in the hallway. "She's detailed all the issues with it, but it sounds like the trap just needs to be cleaned out."

No one responded, and Tam twisted the knob to get out of the house.

"Trey?" Blaine asked, his footsteps coming closer too.

Trey turned back to his brother, and Tam wished she could disappear into one of the lockers in the mudroom.

"I'll do it," Trey said, his voice moving away as he took a few steps. "Your date is here."

"She is?" Blaine asked, and he looked past Trey to Tam. Their eyes met, and Blaine pressed his teeth together so that his jaw jumped. "Tam..." He sighed and stalked toward her.

She turned and went out the door first, the storm that was Blaine not one she wanted to be confined with in a hallway.

"I said I'd come out," he said as he followed her through the garage.

She didn't want to lie and say she didn't get that message, but she couldn't explain why she'd come in either. She just got behind the wheel of her truck and watched as Blaine paused.

"I'm driving," he said.

"I can drive," she said.

He shook his head and walked toward his truck. Tam suddenly wanted to go home. Everything felt like it would be a fight tonight, and she really didn't want to do that. Sighing, she got out of her truck and hurried after him.

"Blaine," she said, "Let's just cancel."

"No," he said over his shoulder. "I'm starving, and I already told my brothers I was going out tonight." He went around to the passenger side of his truck, which was admittedly much nicer than hers, and opened her door.

He didn't smile at her while he waited for her to follow him. Tam paused a few feet away. "I don't want to argue tonight."

"We won't," he said.

"It would've been nice if you'd have told me the rules before I showed up." She gave him what she hoped was a piercing glare and got in the truck.

Blaine turned toward her and leaned into the opening. "I texted."

"I just got it five seconds before I got here," she said. "I didn't think it would be that big of a deal if I came in. I've come in a thousand times."

"Not when I've said I'm going out."

Tam searched his face. "You called it a date."

That strong jaw jumped, but he didn't speak.

"Is it a date, Blaine, or just us meeting to go over the rules of our *fake relationship*?"

He ducked his head, hiding those light brown eyes. He'd

clearly cleaned up for a date, and Tam would've known it had he just come outside after she'd texted or not. She loved his black cowboy hat and the red, white, and blue checkered shirt.

"What was I supposed to tell them?"

"Answer the question."

"Between me and you?" He lifted his eyes to hers. "Or for them?"

"Between me and you," she said, her throat closing. She didn't want to know the truth. She wanted their relationship to be real.

"I said I didn't need rules," he said.

"Yet you made one a few seconds before I got here, and then got all bent out of shape when I broke it."

A few moments of silence passed, and then Blaine nodded. "I suppose that's true." He closed her door and went to get in the driver's seat.

Tension rode with them down the lane to the highway, and Blaine turned toward Lexington, which also led to downtown Dreamsville.

"Tell me what you want, Blaine," she said.

"I..." His voice trailed off, and Tam wished he could just spit it out, as he so often told her to do.

"If there are no rules, you don't get to be mad at me," she said.

"I know," he said.

Tam didn't know what to say next. There were so many confusing things happening between them. He was sending so many mixed messages.

Just tell him.

Tam seized onto the thought and looked out her window. "I'm just going to be honest," she said. "I don't want any rules for this relationship either, because I want it to be real. I want this to be, uh, a real date, and I—" She ground her voice through her throat, determined to fully commit to what she'd started. "I really liked kissing you last night. I can't forget about it, and I can't take back that I said I had a crush on you. If you can forget that, you're so much better than me. I just can't forget that you kissed me and that you'd said you'd been thinking about it for a while. I just can't."

She turned toward him, adding, "Not only that, but you then texted to say you didn't need rules, *especially* not number three, when number three was no kissing. What am I supposed to do with that?"

"I don't know," he said.

"Just be honest with me," she said. "We've always been honest with each other."

"Okay, that's not true," he said. "You've never once told me you had a crush on me."

Tam's frustration increased, bubbling and boiling. "Yeah, well, I do. I do right now, and I did five years ago when I turned thirty and you gave me car mats for my blasted birthday, and I did when I came back from my leatherworking certification, and I did when you graduated from high school." Her chest heaved, but she felt so much lighter now than she had a few minutes ago.

Blaine looked at her for so long, he jerked the truck when

he finally focused on the road again. "I thought you wanted the car mats," he said.

Tam rolled her eyes. "Blaine, you're so blind. Utterly blind." She folded her arms so she wouldn't cry. She would not cry. She would *not*.

"Why didn't you say something?"

"We had an agreement. When I turned thirty, if neither of us was in a relationship, you'd ask me out. I got *car mats*. The message was pretty dang clear, Blaine." She really wanted to get out of this truck, especially when he said nothing. Why didn't *he* say something? Why had he shown up at her house, claiming she'd forgotten him at the house?

"Take me home, please," she said, her voice pitching up.

"No, Tam, come on," he said.

Tam kept her eyes out her window and clenched everything tight to hold the tears back.

"I forgot about the agreement," Blaine said quietly. "If I'm being honest, I'd like this date to be real, and I'm really hoping I didn't mess things up too badly, because I'd really like to kiss you again later tonight."

"Things won't be the same between us," she said.

"I know that," he said. "That's the hardest part about this. That's why I keep going back and forth."

"Maybe it'll be better," Tam said, still unable to look at him.

He reached over and slid his fingers along her forearm until she unfolded her arms and slipped her fingers between his. He squeezed her hand, and with sparks shooting through her body from his touch, she was able to look at him.

He smiled, finally softening into the sexy cowboy she'd been crushing on. They laughed together, and Tam sent up a prayer that a romantic relationship with Blaine would be better than being his best friend.

CHAPTER 22

The hours in Monday, Tuesday, and Wednesday seemed to be double those of a normal day. Neither Benjamin nor Frank had called by five o'clock on Wednesday, and Olli texted Spur to say she didn't need dinner, just ice cream.

He showed up an hour later with Chinese food and four pints of ice cream.

"Bless you," she said as she took the grocery bag with the ice cream.

"Nothing?" he asked. "They didn't call?"

"Not even a text," she said. "No email. No update on the online portal."

"No news is good news," he said.

"How is that true?" she asked, pulling open the silverware drawer to get out spoons.

"Well, they haven't rejected you yet."

Olli supposed that was true. She took out a spoon and

then the pints to see what he'd bought. "Butter pecan—that's for you. Caramel swirl with fudgey brownies. This is for me." She smiled as she opened that container.

Spur smiled at her. "I'm sorry, Olli. I'm sure they'll call tomorrow, and I'm sure you're going to get it. Who could possibly have done better than you?"

"I don't know." Olli took her ice cream to the couch and collapsed onto it with a sigh. "I don't even know who the other finalists were."

"You'd just drive yourself crazy if you did." He stayed in the kitchen, getting out a plate for his food. He came into the living room too and said, "Switch me, baby." He held out a plate of Chinese noodles and the sweet orange chicken she loved, and she handed him the pint of ice cream.

"Thank you," she said, gazing up at him. He seemed to know exactly what to do to take care of her, and she sure did like that. He took the ice cream to the freezer, putting all four pints in before he dished himself a plate of food.

They ate on the couch, and Olli asked him about the horses and the ranch. He talked, though Olli knew he'd rather not. He stayed for a couple of hours, and then he groaned as he got off the couch. "Love you, Olli. They'll call tomorrow, okay?"

"Okay," she said, standing to walk him out.

He took her hand and led her to the door, where he paused. He drew her into his arms and kissed her, and Olli didn't mind so much if she didn't get the grant. She had Spur, and he was the real prize she'd won from all of this.

"Promise me you'll call me first?" he murmured, his lips dropping to her neck.

"Yeah," she said as she breathed out.

"Mm." Spur straightened and looked at Olli, his dark eyes firing with desire. "You want kids, right, Olli?"

"Yes," she said, only mildly surprised by the out-of-the-blue question. They had been talking future plans, as well as revealing some of their hopes and dreams, every night since Saturday.

"But Spur, I'm forty-four already. I'm already pretty late to that game."

"Meaning?"

"Meaning if you wanted kids, and I wanted kids, we'd need to get married and get started on that immediately."

He nodded, his expression turning thoughtful. "Would you be opposed to that course of action?"

Olli blinked, surprised at the line of questioning. They'd talked a little about marriage in the past few days, but Olli had expected to fall more and more in love with him over the course of the next several months. Could she really call her mother and say she was engaged to a man she'd started dating two and a half weeks ago?

"What are you thinking?" he asked.

"I'm trying to decide what I'd tell my mom," she admitted. "You should probably meet my parents before any engaging happens too."

Spur smiled at her, his hand along her hip warm. "Make that happen, Olli."

"I'll call them in the morning," she said. "Fair warning: If you think I'm messy, wait until you see my mother's crafting studio."

"Oh-ho," Spur said, chuckling. "They're retired, right?"

"Yep," Olli said.

"Siblings both married, if I recall."

"Yes," she said again.

"Think about it," Spur said. "I don't want to rush you. I really don't."

"I know." Olli tipped up and kissed him again, then let him go. She watched him walk down the sidewalk and get in his truck. When the headlights broke the darkness, she lifted her hand in a wave, though she couldn't see him anymore.

The next day, Olli did her best to ignore the clock, because the minute hand barely moved at all. She worked on her subscription box advertising in the morning, and then she started packaging the June candles that had been ordered. She'd been scenting and pouring them all week, and when Charity came that evening, they'd get everything labeled and ready for pick-up on Friday afternoon.

Her phone rang just after lunch, and Olli lunged for it and found Benjamin's name there. "Here we go," she said, taking a big breath and pushing it out as she answered the call. "Hello?"

"Olivia," Benjamin said in his round, refined voice. "How are you?"

"Good," she said. "You?"

"I'm well," he said. "Frank wanted to make this call with me, but his daughter is graduating from high school today."

"Wow, that's great," she said. Olli wasn't sure if they both needed to be on the call to let her down easy or to celebrate with her. She paced toward the window she'd left open and through which they'd overheard her and Spur talking. She looked outside, the ranch in the distance.

"Congratulations are in order," Benjamin said. "Olli, we chose you for our gold standard grant."

Olli's smile burst onto her face. As much as she'd coached herself not to squeal, she did. "Thank you, Benjamin. Thank you so much." She laughed, such relief pouring through her. Relief and joy and gratitude. He laughed too, and Olli suspected she was really going to enjoy working with him.

"The gold standard includes product placement in stores," he said. "You'll get the monetary grant requested, and we'll work together to develop one product to put in our stores, with the option for more in the future."

"This is so exciting," she said.

"We want to start with your men's cologne," he said. "Specifically, Spur."

Olli beamed, feeling like actual rays of sunshine were radiating from her very being. "How did your wife like the cologne, Benjamin?"

"She *loved* it," Benjamin said. "I have to say, you've put a smile on a lot of people's faces with that scent. Mine included."

Olli laughed again. "Spur will be thrilled your love life has improved because of him."

Benjamin laughed, and Olli giggled with him. "Thank you," she said again. "Really, thank you so much."

"You're the one with the talent," he said. "I'll send over all the paperwork. Look over it. Have a lawyer look at it. Make sure you're not giving us anything you don't want to give us."

Olli sobered, because she probably should have a lawyer help her with the contracts. "Okay."

"Everything is negotiable," he said. "I never tell people that, which just shows how much I like you." He laughed again, and Olli warmed from the inside out.

She thanked Benjamin one more time and promised she'd be in touch with him about the contracts just as soon as she had her lawyer look them over.

"Your lawyer," she said to herself, still standing in front of that window. "You better get one of those, Olli."

She would, too, after she told Spur the good news.

Olli flew from the perfumery and headed for her car. She drove the few minutes to Bluegrass Ranch, but she wasn't sure where to find Spur on the sprawling estate in the middle of the day. She tried the homestead, and she found one of his brothers—Cayden—there, finishing lunch.

"Do you know where Spur is?" she asked.

"Yeah, he's out at our parents' house."

Olli's excitement would not be hindered by that. "How do I get there?"

"Easy," Cayden said. "You go back down the road toward the highway, but make the first right. Go around the fields to the only house on the lane. You really can't miss it."

"Thank you," Olli said with a big smile. She dashed back to her sedan and did what he said, arriving in the right place only a few minutes later. Spur was indeed there, because his monstrous truck sat in the driveway of a house with a perfectly manicured lawn.

She hurried up the sidewalk to the front porch, where she rang the doorbell. She bounced on the balls of her feet while she waited, and Spur's mother opened the door several moments later.

"Olivia," she said, pure surprise in her voice.

"Hello," Olli said. "I heard Spur was here."

"Yes, we're eating on the upper verandah."

"Could I join you for a few minutes? I just have some amazing news."

"Ma," Spur said. "Let her in." He walked toward them, and his mother made room for him in the doorway. "Olli, what a great surprise." He grinned at her and kissed her.

Olli giggled and said, "Spur, I got it. I got the gold standard, which means they're going to put our cologne in their stores."

"You got it," he repeated, his voice somewhat awed. He laughed and grabbed onto her, lifting her up and spinning her around. "You got it!"

"I got it!" Olli said, laughing. He set her on her feet. "*We* got it, Spur. You're going to be in over four hundred stores across the country."

"Wait a second," his mother said. "What is happening here?"

"I love you," Spur said. "I knew you'd get it. You're too smart and too amazing not to." He touched his forehead to hers, completely ignoring his mother.

"I couldn't have done it without you," she said. "Thank you, Spur."

"Julie?" a man called. "Spur? What are we doin'? Air conditioning all of Kentucky?"

Spur reached into his pocket and dropped to both knees, right there on his parents' porch.

"Oh, Dear Lord," his mother said, pressing one palm to her chest. "Jefferson, he's proposing."

Spur's father appeared, his eyes wide.

"Olivia Hudson," Spur said. "You make me so happy, and I'm in love with you. Will you marry me?" He held up a diamond ring that caught the sunlight even under the eaves of the roof, and nearly blinded Olli.

Her breath had caught in her chest about the time he'd dropped to those knees. "Spur," she gasped. "Really?"

"Absolutely," he said.

Olli felt the weight of three pairs of eyes on her, and she was actually surprised his mother didn't have anything to add to the proposal. She looked at them, and his mom was actually weeping.

She focused on Spur again, her decision crystal clear. "Yes," she said in a strong voice. "Yes, I'll marry you."

His father whooped, and his mom sobbed. Spur got to his feet laughing, and he swooped her into a tight hug. Olli wasn't sure if she should laugh or cry. So much had happened in the space of thirty minutes, and she needed some time to just think.

He slid the diamond on her finger, where they both gazed

down at it. "I love you," Olli said quietly, finally looking up at him. "We're going to have an amazing life together."

"I know we will," Spur said. "I love you, too, Olli." He kissed her, and Olli got the time she wanted to think through how she'd gotten everything she'd ever wanted, all in the space of a few minutes, after many long years of hard work.

* * *

Keep reading for more about Blaine and Tam - the first 2 chapters are included.

Will Tam get out of her own way so she can be with her best friend? Or will old feelings cause a rift between her and Blaine that can't be bridged? **Find out in ROPING THE COWBOY BILLIONAIRE. Available in paperback!**

SNEAK PEEK! CHAPTER ONE – ROPING THE COWBOY BILLIONAIRE

Blaine Chappell rode along the northernmost fence on the ranch, just him, the June Kentucky sunshine, and his horse Featherweight. There was no traffic out there, as there were no roads that bordered this side of the ranch. Only long, straight, white fences, characteristic of every horse farm in the state.

Emerald green grass waved in the slight breeze, and Blaine wished the wind would pick up a little bit to cool him down. He loved Sunday afternoons like this, with the pastor's words flowing through his mind, his thoughts wandering where they wanted, and only a sense of beauty in front of him.

Today, though, his thoughts seemed a little stickier than usual. Featherweight plodded along, her hooves barely kicking up any dust from the grass that had settled in the last week. Blaine felt more at home in the saddle than anywhere else, and had he been shorter, he'd have been the one riding the horses he and his brothers raised to run in the races.

As it was, he oversaw all the medical care of the horses and other animals at Bluegrass Ranch. He'd left the ranch for a couple of years to get his veterinarian technician license for large animals, but the time to invest in veterinary school was too much. The ranch had a team of vets they called on daily, and Blaine didn't need to get the doctorate degree to work with the animals.

He monitored the cattle, the chickens, the sheep, and the goats, as well as the horses. Their main source of income was the championship horses they raised to win the Kentucky Derby, the Preakness, and the Belmont stakes, but there were dozens of other races with tidy prize pots too.

Blaine scheduled all the breeding, and he had seven studs coming in this week to breed with their mares. He, Spur, Duke, and Cayden named every horse, with a lot of the input coming from Cayden, as he was the public face of the ranch. Whoever bought the horse could and usually did rename them, but for a while there, when the Internet headlines ran about the birth of a possible future champion, it was the name the three of them chose.

"What do you think?" he asked Featherweight. "The ones with three or four words sometimes hit the best."

With a gestation period of eleven months, he had plenty of time to pick out names for any foals they might get. There were races for fillies and mares only, some for colts and geldings, and some where they raced against each other.

His favorite race was the Kentucky Oaks, and while most people hadn't heard of it, there was still over a million dollars to be won. Every time a Bluegrass Ranch horse won a race, their bloodlines became more coveted. They could sell their horses for more money.

Spur managed all of that, and Blaine helped when it came time for breeding. They owned one of the former Derby winners who could stud, and that didn't cost them anything. Getting the other males to come to the ranch cost a pretty penny, and besides advertising their two-year-old sale every spring, that was the bulk of the money the ranch spent.

Ian was the numbers brother on the ranch, and Duke was the one who dealt with procuring all the studs. He'd been preparing for this week for the past month, and Blaine had been right at his side for most of that.

He needed to stop thinking about horses, horses, horses. He woke with horses on his mind, and dreamed of horses. He went to bed with horses in his brain, and sometimes he even counted horses when he couldn't fall asleep.

The problem was, if he wasn't thinking about the ranch, his job on it, or horses, he obsessed over Tamara Lennox.

She was ten times as dangerous to let into his mind, especially because he couldn't seem to have an innocent thought about her. She stuck around, needling him, making him question the last two decades of his life. He felt like he'd wasted the last five at least, since she'd turned thirty then, and he'd completely forgotten about their agreement.

She'd reminded him of it last week. They'd agreed that when she turned thirty, if neither of them were in a relationship, he'd ask her out and they'd try something romantic. He'd given her a deluxe set of car mats instead.

"Stupid," he muttered to himself. He'd started dating Alex

about six months after that, and that had been his last relationship. He'd thought it would be his last relationship ever, but Tam had him thinking again.

He could picture her in his mind without even trying. They'd been friends for a little over twenty years, and there was no one on this Earth that he knew better—not even one of his brothers.

He could feel the way her lips pressed against his, as he'd kissed her last week in some insane moment where he'd told Spur to follow his heart, and then Blaine thought he could follow his. If only his heart hadn't led him down such a twisted path.

"She likes you," he told himself, which seemed surreal and natural at the same time. She had admitted to a crush on him, but Blaine still wasn't sure what zone they were in. They'd argued a lot on their last date—which was over a week old now—and he hadn't kissed her when they'd gotten back to the homestead.

She'd thanked him for dinner, and he'd said he'd call her. She'd rumbled away in her beat-up pickup truck, and he'd somehow made it to his suite in the house without encountering another Chappell.

That alone was a miracle, as he'd expected Trey to be lying in wait, a dozen questions on the tip of his tongue.

Trey hadn't said anything to Blaine about going out with Tam. Not one thing. Red flags existed all over that, but this past week had been exceptionally busy at the ranch. Even Duke and Conrad hadn't seen their girlfriends, and Spur had only spent one evening with Olli.

He'd gotten engaged on Thursday night, so he'd had a really busy week.

Blaine had had to hear all about the engagement from his mother when he'd gone for breakfast on Saturday morning. That was probably why Tam had lodged herself in Blaine's mind and refused to be moved out.

"Let's head back," he said to the horse, and Featherweight seemed to understand English. He barely had to point her in the right direction; he just told her where he wanted to go, and she got him there.

He spent a long time brushing her down and cleaning her tack. Once she was back in her stall with a few extra treats in the form of apples and carrots and oats, Blaine started for the homestead. The ranch was massive, spanning hundreds of acres, and they had row houses, walking circles, a full-size track, administration buildings, selling courts and stadiums, arenas, and parking lots for when the buyers came.

There was always someone around, doing something, but Sunday was their slowest day of the week.

Blaine took a long, deep breath, and held it before pushing it from his lungs. Conrad was the best cook out of all the brothers, but Blaine put Sunday evening meals together more than anyone else. Momma usually fed everyone for lunch after church, but she hadn't today, because she and Daddy had gone to see her mother.

Gramma was getting way up there in years, and she lived in an assisted facility in Dreamsville now. Most of the Chappells lived on the ranch until the day they died, and one of Blaine's favorite places was the cemetery.

They buried people on the east half and animals on the west, and some of his favorite childhood pets had been laid to rest on the patch of land in the far eastern corner of the ranch, where the family cemetery sat.

His phone rang as he went past the homestead, his goal the front shed. He had barbells there he liked to work with in the mornings and evenings, and he wanted to check his schedule for the week.

Tam's name sat on his screen, and his feet froze while his heart flopped. He'd texted her quite a bit the past few days, but he hadn't seen her, and he hadn't spoken to her. He quickly swiped on the call when he realized it had rung three or four times already and lifted the phone to his ear.

Tam was swearing, her voice loud, though he could distinctly hear a hissing sound in the background.

"Tam?" he asked.

"Blaine," she barked. "Some idiot ran a stop sign and hit me. Can you come get me?"

His pulse sprinted now, and he jogged toward the homestead. "Yep. Where are you?"

A man said something Blaine couldn't catch, and Tam yelled, "Yes, I called you an idiot. Stop means stop!"

"Tam," Blaine said. "Focus, Tam. Don't engage with him." He could be anyone, and Blaine's worry for his best friend doubled. Inside, he swiped his keys from the hooks inside the mudroom and retraced his steps.

Tam didn't hear him or didn't care what he had to say, because she said something else to the guy who'd hit her.

"You're obviously okay," Blaine said. "At least your mouth."

"I called nine-one-one," she said. "My back hurts."

"Are you sitting down?" Blaine asked, jogging to his truck now. Half of them sat in front of the homestead, as four of the Chappell brothers lived there. The other four lived in a second house further west, and their parents lived on the road that ran along the front of the ranch.

"Yes," Tam said. "I'm fine, Blaine. I'm not going in the ambulance."

"But an ambulance is on the way, right?"

"They're here already," she said. "The police too."

"Then why are you yelling at that guy?"

"He's a police officer, so his buddies are just letting him go wherever he wants."

"Okay, Tamara," Blaine said, employing the use of her full name as he got behind the wheel and started his truck. "Do not yell at a police officer." Especially some of the obscenities she'd been using. "Please."

"I don't feel good, Blaine," she said, and her voice was half the volume and twice the pitch it had just been.

"I'll be right there." He went down the lane that led to the highway at twice the normal clip. "You never told me where you are."

"The stop sign just down from my shop. I got new leather delivered yesterday."

"Which way from your shop, Tam?" he asked, turning left onto the highway. Her shop was near downtown, so he knew he needed to go that way.

"Uh...I don't know," she said.

"Tam," he said. "What's your middle name?"

"Um, Presley?"

Why was she guessing? "Where are the paramedics?" he asked. "You need to get them. You don't sound good, Tam."

"I don't feel good," she said, her voice ghosting into a whisper by the last word.

"Tam," he said, raising his voice. "Tam, which direction from the shop?" He could probably find her pretty easily once he got to her leather-working shop. The flashing lights and emergency vehicles in a small town wouldn't be hard to find.

"Tam?" he asked when she didn't answer. A loud clunk came through the line, and Blaine's blood turned to ice. "Tam," he yelled.

Other voices came through the line, and he heard a man say, "Ma'am? Ma'am, I need you to wake up."

"Hey," Blaine yelled, hoping to get someone's attention.

"Who's this?" a man asked.

"I'm her boyfriend," Blaine said, wearing the label proudly. "Did she pass out?"

"Yes, sir, she did. We've got a team here working with her."

"She said her back hurt," he said. "She was in a car accident about five years ago with her mother." Blaine could still remember getting that phone call too. His anxiety shot through the top of his skull. "She couldn't tell me where she was, and she guessed at her middle name."

"We're at the corner of Leavers and Hoof."

"I'll be there in five minutes," Blaine said. "Or should I meet you at the hospital?"

"We'll still be here in five minutes," the guy said. "I have to go." The line went dead, and Blaine banged his open palm against the steering wheel. He wasn't angry, but frustration looked a lot like anger for Blaine Chappell. So did worry, and that's what was really eating through him.

"I'm coming, Tam," he said under his breath, practically taking a corner on two wheels. "Hang on. I'm coming."

Sneak peek! Chapter Two – ROPING THE COWBOY BILLIONAIRE

T amara Lennox opened her eyes at the touch of someone with cool fingers.

"Tam," he said, and she blinked to be able to see Blaine better. He came into focus slowly, and she tried to sit up.

"Shh, no," he said, pressing that large, cool hand against her shoulder to keep her down. "You're in the back of an ambulance, sweetheart, and you're not getting up."

"No," she said, a powerful sense of choking coming over her. She coughed at the suddenly sterile air. "I said I didn't want to go in the ambulance." Her legs thrashed, and she found them tied down. "Blaine," she said, plenty of panic in her voice. "Help."

But he moved, and another man's face filled her vision. "Ma'am," he said. "It's a six-minute drive, and we're already halfway there."

"No," she said again, desperate now. She couldn't be in an

ambulance. They were so tiny, and she was fine. Even as she thought it, a wave of pain moved down her back. Tears sprang to her eyes.

"I can give you a mild sedative," the paramedic said.

"No," she said again.

"Tam," Blaine said from somewhere. His voice echoed, but she felt it when he slid his fingers between hers. Her body sighed, and some of the panic inside Tam ebbed away. "There you go, baby. Just calm down. They're helping you, not hurting you."

"I don't like ambulances," she whispered. "They're too small."

"You're okay," Blaine said. "You passed out for a minute there, and they had to do something to stabilize your back and neck."

"I said I was fine."

"You're a liar," Blaine said. A moment passed, and he chuckled. Tam found what he'd said funny too, and to her horror, a very girlish giggle came out of her mouth. Maybe they'd already given her something for the pain in her back. Maybe that was why she couldn't feel it anymore.

Another round of anxiety kicked against her ribs. "Don't give me anything," she said. "I don't like drugs." Her voice slurred on the last sentence, and she knew then that she'd already been given something.

Her brain sloshed from side to side as the ambulance turned, and she closed her eyes as a debilitating round of vertigo hit her. "I hate ambulances," she said over and over.

"I hate you, Blaine, for letting them put me in this ambulance..."

* * *

She woke to the sound of Blaine's deep, luxurious voice reading to her from her favorite book. "It doesn't happen all at once. You become. It takes a long time. That's why it doesn't happen to people..."

...who break easily, Tam thought, reciting along with him. Or have sharp edges, or have to be carefully kept. Generally, by the time you are real, most of your hair has been—

"Loved off," Tam said, her voice creaky as she opened her eyes. "And your eyes drop out and you get loose in the joints and very shabby."

Blaine stopped reading, and he met Tam's eyes.

"But these things don't matter at all," she continued. "Because once you are real, you can't be ugly, except to people who don't understand."

A smile bloomed on his face while she finished the page, and he closed the book and set it somewhere out of her sight. "Hey, Tamara." He reached out and stroked her hair off her forehead, and he did it with such love, that she hoped he could love her enough to never think she was ugly, when she grew saggy and old.

She realized then that she wanted to grow old with him, and she wasn't sure how to make that a reality. They hadn't talked much about their actual plan to convince Hayes that they were dating. They'd just been dating. Sort of.

Not really at all, Tam thought. You went on one date, and he didn't even kiss you afterward.

"How do you feel?" he asked, pulling his hand away and folding his arms.

"Okay," she said. "How long have I been out?"

"Oh, like, thirty minutes," he said with a slight scoff. "They did some x-rays and an MRI. I told them they'd be glad you were out for that." He smiled like her claustrophobia was a real hoot.

Tam shivered just thinking about being in that confined pod. "Good thing," she said. "I would've gone crazy."

He nodded. "I'm sorry about the ambulance. They had you loaded before I got there, Tam."

She nodded and tried to sit up further in the hospital bed. "Do I have to stay here?"

"Until the doctor comes back," Blaine said. "At least. I can go let them know you're awake." He got up and moved to the door, which slid open. Tam realized she wasn't in a hospital room, but a little cubicle, and there seemed to be plenty of activity beyond the wall of glass separating her from everyone else.

Someone had drawn the curtains over most of it, but when Blaine stepped out, she heard the chatter, the beeping machines, and the whirring of fans.

Sweat broke out on her forehead, and she flung the blanket off her legs. She wore a hospital gown, and she froze. Someone had undressed her. With fear bumping through her veins, she stared as Blaine came back inside. He slid the door closed and looked at her. "Terrance is coming to check on you."

"Who's Terrance? Where are we? Where are my clothes?"

"Terrance is your nurse," Blaine said without missing a beat. "He's your lead nurse, and nothing gets done unless Terrance says so." He sat back down in the chair he'd been in, a sigh leaking from his mouth. "We're in the ER. Your clothes are in that bag." He indicated a bag on the floor near his feet.

Their eyes met again, and Tam didn't dare ask if he'd seen her undressed. Those milk chocolate eyes buzzed with energy though, like he knew exactly what she was worried about. He said nothing and cocked his head instead.

"Where's your cowboy hat?" she asked.

Blaine reached up and touched his hair, as if he hadn't realized he wasn't wearing a cowboy hat. "I don't know," he said. "I must've lost it somewhere along the way."

"I'm not paying for a replacement," she said automatically. "You have more money than anyone. You cowboy billionaires can buy your own hats."

He laughed, and Tam smiled at the good thing she'd done. "I have plenty of hats, Tam."

"I'm sure you do."

He scooted closer to her and took both of her hands in his. "You sure you're okay? Not feeling dizzy or sick?"

"No," she said.

"Your head doesn't hurt?"

"No," Tam said. "My back either. They gave me something though. I know they did."

"Just a very light sedative," he said. "No painkillers."

"Are you sure?"

"That's what they told me."

Tam wasn't sure if she believed what the doctors told people. When she and her mother had been hit by the twenty-something who'd been texting instead of paying attention to the road, they'd said her mother would make a full recovery. Five years had passed, and she still limped, and she still suffered from neck pain nearly all the time, and her back still went out at least once a week.

She'd been going to the chiropractor religiously every week for years, and Tam didn't think that was a full recovery.

"I just want to go home," she said.

"I'll get you there," he said. "I promise."

"What shape was my truck in?" She watched his reaction, and when he ducked his head, she knew it wasn't good. "You can't hide behind that hat," she teased.

"It's got to be totaled," he said. "The whole front end was smashed up."

"He came out of nowhere," Tam said. "He was going way too fast, and he didn't even slow down for the stop sign." Her blood started to heat. "He's a cop, and I just know he's going to get off with nothing."

"Was he in a police car?"

"No," Tam said. "No lights, no siren, no nothing." She blinked, her thoughts flying through possibilities. "If they say he was, and that the accident was my fault, I won't get insurance money."

"Sure, you will," he said. "You just might have a fee or something."

"Do you know the fee for not yielding to a police officer who has his lights and siren on?" she challenged.

Blaine did not know, and Tam had made her point. "They're not going to do that," he said. "They were taking pictures and stuff when I got there."

"Evidence can be tampered with," she said.

"Okay, Tam," he said with a smile. "This isn't one of your crime dramas."

He hadn't dealt with insurance companies that only wanted to pay the minimum, or who wanted to somehow make a texting college student out to be her mother's fault. She didn't say anything, because she was tired of arguing with Blaine. When they were best friends, it was fun, witty banter. Now that she wanted him to be her boyfriend, the arguments were just annoying.

"Thank you for coming," she said, leaning back into the bed.

He released her hands so he didn't have to lean so far forward. "I will always come when you call, Tam."

Their eyes met, and Blaine rose to his feet slowly. Sparks practically shot out of his eyes, and Tam felt them moving up her arms and into her neck. "I've missed you this week," he said huskily. "We've been so busy on the ranch, and I hate not seeing you." He bent down as if he'd kiss her right there in the emergency room, where the AC clearly wasn't working and she was wearing a white gown with faded, blue flowers on it.

"All right," a man said, his voice easily being broadcast through a microphone. She jumped and looked toward the door while Blaine backed up against the wall. Her heart pounded in her throat and ears as she watched a very large African-American man look up from a clipboard. "Tamara, it's so good to meet you. I'm Terrance."

She had never heard a voice so deep or seen hands so big. She managed to shake his and answer a few questions. He took her temperature and blood pressure, never reporting on what his instruments told him.

He scrawled things on the clipboard and finally looked up. "Are you ready to go home?"

"Yes, please," she said, her voice sounding tinny and quiet.

Lawrence grinned and nodded. "I'll get Doctor Millstone in here to sign you out. Then your boyfriend can take you home and make you comfortable." He turned to Blaine. "She shouldn't be alone tonight. She might have a pretty bad headache, and someone should be there if she starts vomiting or in case she passes out."

"Will she do that?" Blaine asked. "Does she have a concussion?"

"I'll have Doctor Millstone go over the films," Terrance said like the doctor would be handing out brownies. "Her temp is a little elevated, but everyone's is because of the darn air conditioner being out."

Tam knew there'd been a problem with the AC, and for some reason, she felt so proud of herself.

"Otherwise," Terrance said. "She's good." He turned back to her. "Any pain in your head or back? Your neck? Anywhere?"

"Not much," Tam said. "Nothing I'd even take pills for."

"I'm still going to recommend that you go home with

something," he said. "Sometimes our adrenaline covers up pain, and we can't feel it until later." He smiled again, nodded, and left the pod.

Tam looked at Blaine, who looked steadily back. "I'm staying with you tonight," he said.

"I can call my sister."

He grunted, a look of displeasure crossing his face. "I'll have Trey bring me some clothes."

"Yeah, because I'm not going to have anything that fits you."

"Are you calling me fat?" he teased, and a genuine smile flitted across Tam's face.

"You have been eating a lot of peanut butter sandwiches lately."

"It's not the sandwiches that are the problem," Blaine said. "It's all the ice cream I can't stay away from in the evening."

"I have ice cream," Tam said.

"That's why I'm staying with you and not Stacy," he said, grinning at her. He stepped closer again and straightened the chair that he'd knocked sideways when he'd moved away from her. "Do you really hate me, Tam?"

"Did I say that?"

"In the ambulance," he said. "You said you hated me for letting them put you in there."

She looked up at him, and he wore such a vulnerable look on his face. She shook her head. "I could never hate you."

"Never?" His eyebrows went up. "Maybe a real relationship won't ruin our friendship then."

Tam didn't know what to say to that. She knew he'd been

worrying about that for a couple of weeks now. Truth be told, so had she. She couldn't lose Blaine. She'd rather not have him as a boyfriend than lose him completely.

As neither of them had ever had a relationship work out, the likelihood of them remaining friends after all of this was very low. Yet Tam wanted to take the risk. She reached up and cradled his face in the palm of her hand. How could she say everything she felt in her heart and all she thought in her mind?

Turned out, she didn't need to. Blaine leaned down and pressed his lips to hers, and they both said enough with one amazing kiss.

She'll do anything to show her ex she's not still hung up on him...even date her best friend. **You can ROPING THE COWBOY BILLIONAIRE in paperback!**

Bluegrass Ranch Romance

Book 1: Winning the Cowboy Billionaire: She'll do anything to secure the funding she needs to take her perfumery to the next level...even date the boy next door.

Book 2: Roping the Cowboy Billionaire: She'll do anything to show her ex she's not still hung up on him...even date her best friend.

Book 3: Training the Cowboy Billionaire: She'll do anything to save her ranch...even marry a cowboy just so they can enter a race together.

Book 4: Parading the Cowboy Billionaire: She'll do anything to spite her mother and find her own happiness...even keep her cowboy billionaire boyfriend a secret.

Book 5: Promoting the Cowboy Billionaire: She'll do anything to keep her job...even date a client to stay on her boss's good side.

Book 6: Acquiring the Cowboy Billionaire: She'll do anything to keep her father's stud farm in the family...even marry the maddening cowboy billionaire she's never gotten along with.

Book 7: Saving the Cowboy Billionaire: She'll do anything to prove to her friends that she's over her ex...even date the cowboy she once went with in high school.

Book 8: Convincing the Cowboy Billionaire: She'll do anything to keep her dignity...even convincing the saltiest cowboy billionaire at the ranch to be her boyfriend.

Chestnut Ranch Romance

Book 1: A Cowboy and his Neighbor: Best friends and neighbors shouldn't share a kiss...

Book 2: A Cowboy and his Mistletoe Kiss: He wasn't supposed to kiss her. Can Travis and Millie find a way to turn their mistletoe kiss into true love?

Book 3: A Cowboy and his Christmas Crush: Can a Christmas crush and their mutual love of rescuing dogs bring them back together?

Book 4: A Cowboy and his Daughter: They were married for a few months. She lost their baby...or so he thought.

Book 5: A Cowboy and his Boss: She's his boss. He's had a crush on her for a couple of summers now. Can Toni and Griffin mix business and pleasure while making sure the teens they're in charge of stay in line?

Book 6: A Cowboy and his Fake Marriage: She needs a husband to keep her ranch...can she convince the cowboy next-door to marry her?

Book 7: A Cowboy and his Secret Kiss: He likes the pretty adventure guide next door, but she wants to keep their relationship off the grid. Can he kiss her in secret and keep his heart intact?

Book 8: A Cowboy and his Skipped Christmas: He's been in love with her forever. She's told him no more times than either of them can count. Can Theo and Sorrell find their way through past pain to a happy future together?

TEXAS LONGHORN RANCH ROMANCE

Book 1: Loving Her Cowboy Best Friend: She's a city girl returning to her hometown. He's a country boy through and through. When these two former best friends (and ex-lovers) start working together, romantic sparks fly that could ignite a wildfire... Will Regina and Blake get burned or can they tame the flames into true love?

Book 2: Kissing Her Cowboy Boss: She's a veterinarian with a secret past. He's her new boss. When Todd hires Laura, it's because she's willing to live on-site and work full-time for the ranch. But when their feelings turn personal, will Laura put up walls between them to keep them apart?

About Emmy

Emmy is a Midwest mom who loves dogs, cowboys, and Texas. She's been writing for years and loves weaving stories of love, hope, and second chances. Learn more about her and her books at www.emmyeugene.com.

Printed in Great Britain
by Amazon

19186071R00161